Rutherford's WOMAN
A Family Legacy

A NOVEL BY
L. J. BOWEN

Copyright © 2018

Published by Major Key Publishing

www.majorkeypublishing.com

ALL RIGHTS RESERVED.

Any unauthorized reprint or use of the material is prohibited. No part of this book may be reproduced or transmitted in any form or by any means, electronic, or mechanical, including photocopying, recording, or by any information storage without express permission by the publisher.

This is an original work of fiction. Names, characters, places and incidents are either products of the author's imagination or are used fictitiously and any resemblance to actual persons, living or dead is entirely coincidental.

Contains explicit language & adult themes suitable for ages 16+

JOIN IT'S MAJOR

To submit a manuscript for our review, email us at submissions@majorkeypublishing.com

SYNOPSIS

William Rutherford is a pre-law student at Howard University who comes from a wealthy family. He's making his own way in life and not letting his background and wealth dictate his path. Nursing major, Jemma Alden, comes from a humble background, and Will has been enthralled with her since their first year of school. They realize they have a lot in common, as far as experiencing tragedies at a young age, after discussing their past, families, and hopeful futures.

Outside forces in the form of a classmate and family member test the newfound relationship by inserting themselves into the couple's life and becoming an adversary toward Jemma. After a disastrous dinner with Will's grandparents, the couple reevaluate their feelings, and their relationship is consummated for the first time. As the bond continues to prosper, a family fundraiser allows Felicia to execute a plan to break up the couple, and Will is hospitalized. With the aid of Will's brother, they search for answers, and with interference from Mona, Jemma misunderstands the situation and decides to leave school. Will scouts for Jemma so they can talk and work things out, but after three months of no contact from her, Will gives up.

"Because I was trying to figure out why the hell she drugged me! You of all people should have known that picture was fake. I didn't have any interest in Felicia. I loved you, Jemma, only you."

— -WILL RUTHERFORD

ACKNOWLEDGMENTS

I would like to thank Danielle Southern for being my extra set of eyes and giving me ideas to think outside the box. My thanks are also extended to Alyson Reynolds for the phone conversations, endless messages, and patience for answering all of my questions.
To my twin sister and biggest supporter, Ashira, thank you for being my better half and my rock.
Last, but never least, I want to thank God for giving me the creativity and imagination called writing.

CHAPTER 1

HOWARD UNIVERSITY, 1983

William Rutherford sipped the last of his coffee as his eyes followed his favorite waitress around Chit Chat's, the most popular hangout spot on campus. It served as a calm getaway for studying and as a rowdy location after sporting events. The eatery had a 1950's diner style sight to it, by having black and white tile flooring with mint green and white booths that were perched alongside the windows. Matching chrome and vinyl table and chair sets also filled the space that had a Pac-Man arcade game in one corner and an authentic jukebox in another corner. Behind the register, it had a countertop cooler that held the old school soda bottles, and a rectangle-shaped chalkboard was resting on a tripod by the door that displayed the day's special. It was a Wednesday night, and Will had decided to take advantage of the quiet by studying for his English exam. Aside from the ambience, Will liked it because of the cute server with hazel eyes. She was shorter than him and had dimples with mocha skin. Her hair was pulled back into a loose bun, and he liked watching her interacting with the people in the diner. He wouldn't be a man if he didn't appreciate her fine, womanly figure through her purple and gray uniform. He knew she had a nice, round backside with just the right amount of hips and breasts. Will's eyes were downcast, and he was so busy daydreaming that he didn't see Jemma approach the booth.

"Can I take your plate?" she asked, looking at the empty dishes that once held a grilled cheese sandwich and fries.

"Oh, sure. Thanks."

"You're welcome. Would you like a refill?"

"Yes, that'll be great."

He watched as she trotted away, his eyes glued to her legs. *Damn, she's cute!* Will was a tall, athletically built sophomore, with a square cut jaw, Swiss chocolate coloring, and green eyes that he and his brother, Robert, had inherited from their mother. Students and teachers often mistook him for an upper classman because of his height and wide frame, which was why he was the second-string quarterback for the football team.

"There you go," Jemma said as she refilled his cup with a fresh pot of coffee.

"Thanks again."

"You're welcome. Can I get you anything else?"

"No, I'm fine. Is it cool if I stay here and study?" Will knew it was, but he wanted to extend the conversation with her. He sat back in the booth to gaze at her, hazel eyes meeting green eyes.

"Sure. Most students come in here to study anyway, and you're lucky because it's not crowded tonight."

"Guess I better use that to my advantage, huh?"

"It wouldn't hurt," she replied, and he laughed.

"What are you studying?" she asked out of curiosity, still holding the coffee pot.

"African-American Lit."

"Really? I wanted to take that class, but it was full. Professor Ashton, right?"

"Yes, and she's extra serious about it. We have a test every week."

"Well, you seem like a smart guy. I'm sure you can handle it."

Jemma walked away after their brief conversation, returning to the customers at the counter. He stared at her for a few more minutes before opening his textbook. Jemma spared a glance at Will as she wiped the crumbs off the countertop. She wanted to see if he was watching her again, and it also gave her the chance to check him out. She'd noticed that he started coming into Chit Chat's toward the end of freshman year and had to admit he was a handsome one. He was so fine with his physique, a smile to die for, and his green eyes were irresistible. She knew the female population was going crazy over him, and the fact he played football was a bonus. Jemma had written for the school paper last year, and she knew all about the Rutherfords. His grandparents were alumni, and she had written the story when they made a huge donation to upgrade the library and student activities building. They came from old money and had plenty of it. If she remembered correctly, the family made their money from manufacturing computers. She glanced at the clock and let out a deep breath.

Two more hours and she'd be off until Friday. There was a basketball game Saturday night, and if Howard won, the place would be packed afterwards. She loved these slow days because she could keep up with everything that had to be done and not run herself ragged. On the weekends, there were three other waitresses, and they rotated during the week. Jemma's tuition had been paid in full, but she liked working to keep extra money in her bank account. Jemma looked at Will again, and her face softened when she saw he was into his book. The bell above the door jingled, and she went to greet the customers. When Will got up an hour and a half later to leave, he'd left a five-dollar tip, knowing he'd be back soon.

The September night was brisk as he hunched up the collar of his leather jacket. He loved the beauty of the campus regardless of the season. The grass was always mowed and free from trash. He never had to worry about his safety because the quad was nicely lit, and campus police were always on patrol. While walking home, he passed a few students and teachers who were also trying to get to their destinations and out the cold weather. Once he reached his apartment, he headed toward his room to take a long, hot shower and relax for the rest of the night.

Jemma walked into her room at Bailey Hall and saw her roommate and best friend, Sonya, sitting at the desk studying with the record player spinning a Jackson 5 album. The dormitory housed the flat style complexes that had the feel of a dorm by having a RA but was designed like an apartment. It was a long, spacious area that had a gray linoleum floor that had a dark blue oblong rug. It had a living room/dining room combo, with a small sink and stove. The TV set on stacked milk crates that were covered by a sheet that had blue birds on it, and the radio was sitting on a low table next to the crates. They had to share a bathroom but had their own room. It was big enough for a wooden desk, dual three-tiered dresser inside the closet, and a twin-size bed. They each had their room decorated to their taste, and luckily, neither one was a messy person. The room was on the third floor, so they could leave the curtains open without having to worry about a peeping Tom. Jemma and Sonya had to dish out extra funds to reside there since it usually catered to upper classmen, but they didn't mind paying for the extra incentives.

"Hi."

"Hey, working lady. You look tired."

"I am."

"I don't know why you're busting your hump working as a waitress?"

"It's only a part-time job, and I don't have the luxury of calling my daddy whenever I need money." Sonya stuck her tongue out at Jemma and went back to her notebook. Sonya's dad was an up and coming politician, and her mom was a homemaker. Sonya was the same height as Jemma with a darker complexion and was donning a fresh finger wave hairstyle. Those were true words that Jemma had spoken to Sonya. Her parents died in a boating accident while on a romantic getaway when she was ten years old and had been raised by her mother's sister, Paris. Whenever the school had family weekends, it hit Jemma hard that her parents would never get to see their daughter all grown up at college, but she knew they were with her in spirit, and that always eased the heartache. Jemma changed into a pair of green shorts and a t-shirt.

"Ugh! I smell like grease. By the way, I like your new hairstyle."

"Thanks. It was my first time going to that new salon, and I liked the stylist, Linda. She said she'd give me a discount the next time I go if I bring a friend, so hint hint…" Jemma nodded at that, knowing she could take a day and treat herself to a trip to the boutique. Sonya had on a pink and yellow jumpsuit with matching socks.

"So, are you going to the game on Saturday night?" Sonya asked, closing her book and packing her bookbag for the next day.

"No, I have to work."

"Jeez! You never have any fun, Jemma."

"I do have fun. Didn't I join you on that double date last weekend?"

"We were home by 9:30!"

"It wasn't my fault the guy was a sexist jerk." Sonya chuckled and got up to sit on the couch, pushing the bookbag to the side.

"All I'm saying is we're sophomores at an excellent university. We're smart, young, and beautiful; don't let the college experience go by without enjoying it. Date. Go to frat parties. Stay out past curfew."

"I *am* enjoying college life, Sonya."

"So, come with me to the game. Doesn't that chick with the afro owe you since you covered for her a few weeks ago? Cash in the favor."

"All right. You're such a pain in the butt." Sonya laughed and went back to the desk, both girls singing along with Jermaine Jackson.

JEMMA DID INDEED ASK Leah to return the favor and ended up going to the game with Sonya and some other girls from the dorm. Sonya wore black leggings with an oversized off the shoulder shirt while Jemma had on a stone washed blue jean skirt with a purple shirt; her L.A. Gears completed the outfit by having matching shoe strings. It was half time, and Howard was up by seven. The girls were in the line for the concession stand and the crowd around them was excited and talking loudly. The cheerleaders were doing their half-time show and keeping the audience entertained.

"Having fun?" Sonya asked Jemma.

"Yes. Thanks for being pushy and getting me to switch my night."

"You're welcome," she replied with a smug look on her face. Jemma, all of a sudden, felt goose bumps cross her skin. She looked around until she saw Will standing a few feet away, looking at her. He was standing with a group of guys with some of them wearing letterman jackets. She didn't know why, but she got excited when she saw him excuse himself and head her way.

"Can you get me something to drink, please? I'll be right back," she told Sonya as she got out of line and met Will halfway.

"Hello."

"Hi. How did your test go?"

"Not too bad. I got a B+." She nodded with an easy smile.

"Congrats."

"Thank you for asking." Will wore a red Howard hoodie with blue jeans.

"Let me formally introduce myself. My name is William Rutherford, but you can call me Will." He held out his hand, and she looked at it before taking it.

"Jemma Alden. Nice to meet you." When she touched his big hand, Jemma literally felt a sharp energy run up and down her body, and her skin prickled.

"Likewise. It's good to see you outside the diner," Will said and Jemma chuckled.

"Yeah, who are you telling?"

"You look nice tonight." She flushed at his words, and he was surprised by the act. *How many girls still blushed?*

"Thank you."

"You're welcome."

"I think your friends are waiting for you," she said, nudging in the direction of his group.

"They're cool. If you don't mind me asking, what are you doing after the game?"

"Going back to my dorm to study. I have a math test on Monday. Why?"

"I was going to ask you if you wanted to grab a bite to eat," he replied, and she was mildly shaken. It had been a while since she'd been on a genuine date, and it certainly wasn't with a guy of Will's caliber.

"Like a date?" He nodded, and a frown appeared between her brows. *Why would a Rutherford ask me out?* Jemma, without being conceited, knew she was pretty with a good personality. But the Rutherfords dated high society... they always did.

"Umm..."

"You seem surprised that I want to take you out."

"Well, to be honest, I am. You're a Rutherford. Shouldn't you be dating the Tiffany Van Smythe-Kennedy's of the world?" Will slowly nodded his head, running his hand down his chin. This was a first... being turned down because of his name and all that came with it. He wasn't mad; he was just bothered that Jemma wasn't willing to get to know what type of person he was.

"I'm not like that, Jemma. Thank you for voicing your preconceived notions about me." His eyes showed his offended feelings, and Jemma felt bad for placing them there. He walked away from her and went back to his buddies.

"Will, wait!" He kept walking, and Sonya appeared next to her.

"Here's your water. What's wrong?" Sonya asked, seeing a tall guy walk away from her best friend.

"I just stuck my foot in my mouth. C'mon, let's go back to the game." Howard ended up winning by twelve points, and the girls walked back to the dorm; the campus was in good spirits due to the victory.

JEMMA DIDN'T SEE Will until the following Saturday at Chit Chat's. She had walked back from the kitchen and saw him sitting at the counter.

"Hi, Will."

"Hey, Jemma."

"I'm glad you came in. I wanted to apologize for what I said to you at the game. I don't make assumptions about people, and I shouldn't have done it with you. I'm sorry."

Will looked at her for a full minute then he let out a small grin. He knew she meant the words and was glad that she was willing to admit she had jumped to conclusions regarding him.

"Apology accepted. I really do like you, Jemma. I've wanted to ask you out since last year. But I don't want my family's money to be an issue."

"You don't know anything about me, Will," Jemma replied, her hands on her hips.

"I know that you're a hard worker. You like sports, you're studious, and you have beautiful eyes. I want to get to know you better; is that a crime?" She unconsciously bit her bottom lip at his question, and Will found that habit sexy as hell.

"Excuse me? Can I have a refill?" a student at the end of the counter asked, lifting his empty soda glass. Jemma went to replenish the soft drink and went around to the other patrons to make sure their dining needs were taken care of.

"No, Will, it's not a crime. I'm just not used to a guy like you asking me out."

She didn't know why she was saying this to him, but there was something inside Jemma prompting her to be open with Will.

"This isn't high school, Jemma. We're both adults. What kind of guys are you used to?" he asked, and she shrugged. She could tell by his facial expression he was into the conversation and wanted her to be honest with him.

"Guys who like to hit the books, are in a lot of clubs. Guys who—"

"Sounds like you like nerds."

"There's nothing wrong with nerds." She chuckled.

"Did you want something off the menu?"

"Cheeseburger, fries, and a chocolate milkshake." Jemma went to place the order and cleaned a couple of tables from where some customers had left.

"How was your Math test?" Will asked her as she walked back to the counter.

"It was OK. I passed it."

"What is your major?"

"Nursing. You?"

"Criminal Justice. My goal is to be a lawyer."

"If you don't mind me asking, why wouldn't you go into your family business?" Jemma asked with her hands in her apron pockets, hoping she hadn't overstepped a personal boundary with him. Will cleared his throat and shrugged his shoulders.

"It never appealed to me. I mean, I know it was probably expected of me to pick up the reins since I'm the oldest, but being a lawyer has always fascinated me. It's something about the workings of the law and being a proponent for innocent people that pulls at me."

She nodded at that, liking his answer as she looked around the diner. She was surprised that it wasn't busy like the usual Saturday nights. But then again, the Greek showcase was taking place in the auditorium, which was considered the kick-off for the homecoming celebration in a few weeks. There were only six people in the diner, including Will and Jemma. She brought his food out and stepped back while he ate.

"How did your family take the news that you wanted to be a lawyer?" Will took a long sip of his milkshake before answering.

"My grandfather was fine with it, but my grandmother wants me to reconsider, but I refuse. The company has a board of directors they can trust to keep things afloat."

"I bet she wasn't too happy to hear about your plans," Jemma said, getting absorbed into his green eyes and the discussion they were having.

"Don't get me wrong, I love my grandmother, but she's set in her ways. She figures since the Rutherford men started the company, my brother and I should just dive right in and take care of it. In addition to that, she's old-fashioned and still goes by the brown paper bag of colorizing black folks. She's a snob, and I've told her many times. She never forgave my dad for marrying my mother. They were in love, and that's all that mattered."

Jemma poured herself a glass of water, liking the fact that he was talking to her about his family... even if some of what he had revealed was a little outrageous.

"You said were. Did they get a divorce?" He pushed his plate away and took a deep breath before continuing. Will didn't mean to venture down that path, but it was a small part of him that didn't balk at what he was about to tell her.

"No. Some guy tried to rob them as they were leaving the movies one night. My dad, being the man that he was, tried to fight the guy off, and he shot both of my parents."

He told the story in a low, gruff voice. He honestly hated talking about what happened, but he was told that discussing it—letting it out was therapeutic, instead of letting the anger, animosity, and grief build up inside him. No one in his family knew, but sometimes he'd go to the local gym and spend hours hitting the punching bag to release his bad feelings about his parents' deaths.

"I am very sorry, Will." Jemma's eyes were filled with sorrow, and he also saw a bit of sadness as well. He nodded, sipping his drink.

"Did they find the man who did it?" Jemma asked after a discomforting silence grew between them.

"Yes. The sun will burn out before he is released from prison."

"Well, that's good."

"Yeah. He won't be able to hurt anyone else, but it won't bring my parents back."

That whole ordeal was one of the reasons that prompted him to go into law; to protect the innocent people in the world and to seek fairness for them. Justice had been served for his parents, and he wanted to make his mark in the world as being someone who continued to enforce it. Jemma nodded, feeling his rage and pain. She was all too familiar with those emotions, and although they would never go away, taking it day-by-day made it easier to manage.

"I understand how you feel, Will," she said softly, and she gasped at his sudden outburst.

"No, you don't! You have no damn idea—"

"My parents died when I was younger, too. They were killed in a boating accident. They were on a romantic getaway and wanted to take a midnight cruise along the lake. The waterfront hotel where they were staying offered that service, and they didn't know that the guy who did the tours had been drinking. He crashed the boat into some rocks, and it exploded on impact. So, I know how mad and pissed you are regarding your parents' untimely passing."

Will wanted to kick himself as Jemma went to clean off the vacant, dirty tables. It was just him in the place, the cook and owner clanging away in the kitchen.

"Jemma, you OK?" Danny, the chef, asked after she'd placed the bin of dirty dishes in the kitchen so they could be washed.

"Yes, I'm fine, Danny. It's just one customer."

She went to where he was sitting and took away the plate and glass. He noticed that she was tense after what she'd just said, and he couldn't blame her for being weary right now.

"I'm sorry, Jemma."

"It's all right, Will," she replied, gnawing at her bottom lip again.

"It seems like we keep apologizing to one another," he mentioned, and she snickered.

"That, we do."

"If you're not busy tomorrow, would you like to have dinner with me?" Will asked, and she cleared her throat before answering.

"I would love to, but I have a standing appointment with my aunt Paris every Sunday. We go to church then she cooks a big dinner."

"That sounds great," Will said in a distant voice. She cleared her throat and decided to take a leap of faith.

"Would you like to join us? I mean, I don't know your religious preference, but—"

"I'd love to. If it means we can spend some time together, yes." She smiled softly at his words, looking up when a few people walked in.

"You don't have to worry. My aunt won't give you the third degree about anything," she lightly warned before heading to the new customers.

CHAPTER 2

Will looked up after Aunt Paris finished saying grace and grinned at the scene before him. When Will had walked into the cozy house, he was hit by a cluster of enticing scents that made his mouth water. Baked macaroni and cheese, black eyed peas, cornbread, and smothered chicken with homemade lemonade had been prepared for dinner. It had been a while since Will had a meal like this, and he was looking forward to it. Aside from him, Jemma, and her aunt, they were joined by Paris's beau, Stan. The older couple were too funny to Will and had made him laugh.

They bickered like a married couple but flirted like teenagers. He had met them in front of Paris's church, Higher Mountain Baptist, wearing a brown suit with matching shoes and a white tie. Jemma was wearing a navy skirt with a white blouse and kitten heels.

"This smells so good, Paris," Stan said as the food was passed around.

"Thanks, darling. You're still doing the dishes though." Stan made a look like she'd hurt his heart, and Jemma grinned.

Stan had been in the picture since she had moved to live with her aunt after the accident, and she looked at him as a father figure. They absolutely adored each other, and she was glad for the consistency they provided in her younger years.

"Now, don't be shy, Will. Jemma told me she was bringing a guest home, and I cooked all my goodies," Paris said to him while pouring some lemonade in her glass.

"No, ma'am. All this good food, I'm coming back for seconds."

"Now, that's what I want to hear. Jem, baby, how's school?" Paris asked, eating some cornbread. She was of average height for a woman, the same complexion as Jemma, with a bob haircut and a slim build.

"It's going good, Auntie."

"Will, what's your major, if you don't mind me asking?" Stan inquired, partaking in the conversation.

"Criminal Justice, sir. I plan to specialize in law."

"Oh, that's good. Maybe by the time you be a lawyer, you can recommend a good judge to marry me and Paris."

"Oh, hush, Stan," she said with a soft chuckle.

He was a tall dark-skinned man who resembled Isaac Hayes but with hair. Will chuckled and looked at Jemma who had a content look on her face. Dinner continued with easy talk and laughs while warm cinnamon apple pie with coffee was served as dessert. Afterwards, Jemma and Will sat on the enclosed porch while the older people did the dishes.

"I feel like we should help your aunt and Stan in the kitchen," Will stated as he and Jemma sat on the long porch swing, Jemma wrapping a sweater around her shoulders.

"Aunt Paris said they're fine. Besides, they're probably in there kissing at the sink," Jemma replied with a soft chuckle.

He got the swing going with a kick of his foot, and they quietly enjoyed the comfortable silence. She wasn't as nervous as she thought sitting here with Will. It was a calm stillness as they sat next to each other, enjoying the sights and sounds of the tree-lined street. The other houses were similar in design to Paris's, and there were some with a few modifications. When the breeze shifted, she was able to get a whiff of his strong cologne. It was a tangy, woodsy aroma, and it seemed to fit his body chemistry.

"Thank you for inviting me, Jemma." He broke the quietness, and she nodded.

"You're welcome. Did you have a good time?"

"Yes, those two are a trip," he answered, jerking toward the kitchen, and she agreed with a grin.

"But seriously, this was nice. Sunday dinner with my grandparents is always a formal affair with the servants dishing out elaborate food in the big dining room," Will mentioned, giving her another indication of his life.

"Is there at least conversation at the table?"

"After the talk of school, my grandmother usually monopolizes the meal about her latest fundraiser or whose grandchild got married in her circle of haughty friends." She watched him talk, having empathy for him.

Growing up in a household with a grandmother like that… She was lucky she had had her aunt to raise her after the accident. Jemma's mom and her sister had very similar features, and it almost seemed like her mother was always around.

"How could you stand that when you were younger?"

"My brother and I had each other, and we kept up the mischief," he replied with a laugh.

"Boys will be boys, huh? What's his name?"

"Robert. He's a freshman, and we share an off-campus apartment with our friend Brandon."

"Does he rebel against your grandmother as well?"

"Oh yes! She wants him to be a doctor, and he drives her crazy by telling her he's a theater major." Jemma laughed at that, and he liked the sound.

"Are you playing for homecoming?" she asked him softly since she knew he was the second string running back for the football team.

"I'm not sure, but I'll suit up. Why? You gon' come to the game and watch me play?"

"Oh, you'd like that, wouldn't you?" she asked with a slight smirk.

He quickly responded, "Yes, I would Jemma." She looked at him, taken aback by his assured words.

"I would, but I have to work that night. It's going to be crazy, especially if we win."

"Well, you might as well prepare because we're going to win."

"You're a cocky lil' thing, aren't you?" she asked with an amused look.

"No. Just stating a fact." She smiled at that, their eyes meeting again over the easy dialogue.

Will looked at his watch and saw it was 8:20. "Are you ready to go?" she asked as he stood up.

"It's getting late. I don't want you to rush getting ready for class tomorrow morning."

"That's considerate. Thank you."

"You're welcome." As they prepared to leave, Paris made Will a to-go plate and said goodbye to the adults after thanking Jemma's aunt for having him over. Stan and Paris waved to them from the doorway as Will drove them back to campus in his Jaguar Roadster.

THE CAMPUS WAS BUZZING with excitement for homecoming week. Alumni were visible and making themselves known by trying to show up the youngsters with their stories and outfits. Just like Jemma predicted, Chit Chat's was busy the day of the game. She had to admit it was nice to walk through the campus and see the team spirit visible with balloons and streamers on several buildings and people walking around in school colors. There were three other waitresses working, and Danny had extra help in the kitchen. Jemma clocked in at 5 p.m. and headed toward her section of tables toward the back of the restaurant.

Meanwhile at the football game, it was half time, and Will was getting hyped at the coach's encouraging words in the locker room. Other players were sitting down, nodding at the speech, and some of the defensive players were jogging in place and moving their hands up and down to keep their limbs loose. The star running back had gotten hurt in the last play, and it was Will's time to shine since they were down by three points. In an overtime game, Will had caught the ball from the quarterback in a rush play and ran the ball to a touchdown causing Howard to win the football game. The crowd exploded with cheers and claps as they and the marching band rushed the field to celebrate with the team and cheerleaders. They didn't even get a chance to shake hands with the other team because there was so much excitement going on, and the press was there, trying to get quotes from the coach and some key players.

An hour and half later, Jemma had picked up a tray of sodas and headed toward a large group sitting in the back booth. They were from the losing team and had been obnoxious since coming in after leaving the stadium. She had to weave around the crowd in the diner, catching animated conversations here and there. Jemma has happy that Howard had won and knew the rest of the weekend was going to be hyped with all the parties and get togethers. There were ten guys total in the booth, and a big guy named Felix was the ring leader. Jemma thought he was a brainless ape due to his behavior, but she kept her opinion to herself.

"Here are your drinks. Have you all decided on what you want?" Jemma asked, passing out the cold beverages.

"Yeah... you butt naked on a bed," Felix said, and the other guys at the table laughed. She placed her hand on her hip and looked at him.

"That's not on the menu, and if you keep making comments like that, I'm going to have you kicked out of here."

"Whatever you say." He reached out and tugged on the bottom of her uniform.

"Stop that!" she hissed, pushing his hand away.

"C'mon, stop being such an uppity bi—" Before Jemma knew what had happened, Felix's head was slammed down on the table with his left arm wretched behind him and the left wrist was being held at an odd angle. She stared with wide, shocked eyes as Will bent Felix's wrist back further, causing the guy to groan with pain.

"Now, I do believe the lady asked you to stop being inappropriate with her, right?" Jemma didn't see Will walk in with some other football players and cheerleaders.

It had gotten quiet as people stared at the scene in awe, some of the other patrons were getting ready to throw down if the troublemakers wanted to go that route. Jemma looked at Will bend the wrist back further, his other arm pressed down on Felix's head.

"Speak up!"

"Yes, she did," Felix responded with an unmanly whine.

"Apologize right now," Will growled in a low, menacing voice.

"I'm sorry for being inappropriate with you."

"Jemma, are you OK with his apology?" Will asked her, breaking the spell he'd cast when he looked at her. She nodded with wide eyes, and he looked down at the jerk.

"You're lucky she said yes. Now get the hell out of here!" Will pushed him toward the door, and Felix left with his crew, and some people applauded.

"Turn the music up! Let's celebrate!" someone shouted and got a loud response as "Celebration" by Kool & the Gang boomed from the jukebox. Will saw Jemma head to the back, and he followed her. She was in the storage room, leaning against the metal shelves when he walked in.

"Hey. Are you OK?" he asked, standing across from her as he closed the door behind him. She cleared her throat, nodding.

"Yes. I'll be out in a few minutes."

"It's no rush." He reassured her with calm eyes.

"Thank you for what you did, Will. I appreciate it."

"You're welcome. I don't why I just snapped when I saw him reaching for you."

She nodded again, unable to look away from him. To be honest, Will wanted to break his damn arm for what he did, but he wasn't going to let the asshole ruin the mood of the night.

"Congrats on winning the game," Jemma softly told him, still holding eye contact with Will.

"Thanks. I'm sure all the details will be in the school newspaper."

"I'll be sure to grab a copy." He bowed his head again as Jemma smoothed out her uniform before leaving the room. They continued to stare at each other, the air between them crackling with electricity and vibrant wanting. She thought he looked so good in dark jeans and his sports jacket.

"Thanks again," she mumbled, licking her lips, knowing she probably sounded like a goof by repeating the same words.

Will's eyes saw her glistened lips, and the last string of his control snapped. "Aw, the hell with it."

Will grabbed Jemma by the waist and pulled her to him, then he lowered his head to kiss her. It wasn't a gentle peck either. It was an intense, extraordinary, and beyond fantastic kiss, and she felt it all the way to her core. His tongue added to the mix, and it was causing all types of madness within her. She wrapped her arms around his neck, deepening the embrace. One hand slowly ran up her spine to cup the back of her head, keeping it angled right where it was so he could continue to taste her plump, juicy mouth. They didn't know how long they were kissing, but they both knew it shouldn't end any time soon. She ran her thumb across his jaw just as a loud knock sounded on the door.

"Breaks over, Jemma. Let's go!" Danny said as he pounded on the door again. She stepped back from Will, moistened her lips in a deliberate motion, and quickly left the room. *What in the hell was that?* Will thought to himself, mindful of his racing pulse and pounding erection.

SONYA LOOKED AT JEMMA, who was in a thoughtful daze, as the two were in the library studying on a cold, rainy night. It was a four-story building that had a rustic yet updated look to it. There was a tall ceiling with a domed glass and a white crisscross pattern design. The tables were a light oak color and had small lamps with a plastic white shade. The shelves were fully stocked with all types of periodicals, and the banister was open so that one could glimpse down to the tables and check-out desk. It was a week after homecoming, and things were back to normal on campus. Jemma was working on her debate topic but kept getting sidetracked by the memory of Will's kiss. That sweet, tingling, oh-so delectable—

"So, you gonna do that, Jemma?" Sonya asked with a smile on her face, breaking into her friend's musings.

"Hmm, yeah. That sounds like fun." Sonya laughed, and a few students from other tables looked at her. She threw a pencil at Jemma, who looked at her best friend.

"What?"

"I just asked if you would get a tattoo that said, 'George Michael for President' and you said that would be fun." She laughed and gave Sonya her pencil back.

"I'd vote for him to be president."

"Well, seeing as though he's from England, that might be a problem."

"My mind was elsewhere... Sorry."

"I see. You want to talk about it?" Sonya asked, playing with her writing utensil.

Jemma let out a deep breath, sitting back in the chair. "You remember that guy I was talking to at the game?"

"That six-foot-tall, handsome hunk of man flesh? Yes." She smiled before retelling what happened at Chit Chat's, and Sonya covered her heart with her hand.

"That is so sweet! I can't believe he did that."

"He kissed me afterwards," Jemma blurted out and smiled at Sonya's facial expression.

"Wait. Did he regular kiss you or *kiss* kiss you?" Sonya asked with raised eyebrows.

"The second one."

"Well, c'mon, how was it? I want details."

"It was—" Jemma let out a deep breath, flushing at the memory. "It was awesome, fantastic. He's an amazing kisser."

"Wow. I've never seen you blush before. Must've been as sweet as you say. Is he your boy toy now?"

"No! I don't know. I mean, we haven't even been on a date yet."

"Maybe you two should discuss it because here he comes." Sonya nudged her head toward Will, and Jemma turned around to look.

He was walking toward their table, and she felt her heart flutter, unable to stop the spontaneous movement. He was wearing jeans and a black turtleneck under his jacket with his book bag slung over one shoulder.

"Hello, ladies," he said, leaning forward on his hands on an empty chair.

"Hi, Will."

"Hello. Sonya Augustine. Nice to meet you," Sonya introduced herself, and he took her hand in a quick shake.

"Same here. Will Rutherford." He shook her hand, his eyes going back to Jemma.

Sonya looked between the two and got up with a grin on her face, gathering up her things. "Well, I'm going to take off. Looks like a deep conversation is about to happen." Jemma smiled when Sonya pointed to Will behind his back and gave a thumbs-up sign. He sat across from Jemma, and they eyeballed each other for a few minutes.

"How have you been?" she asked, deciding to break the ice.

"Good. You?"

"The same; just catching up on some work."

"What are you studying?" he asked, nodding toward her index cards.

"I'm just making notes for my debate meeting."

"So, you're a full-time student, a part-time waitress, and on the debate team? You're just a regular renaissance woman, aren't you?" She shrugged with a smirk, giving him a side glance that Will found very cute.

"When's the debate?"

"In a few days. We're going against St. Trinity."

"You'll do great." She welcomed his words, nervously playing with the top of her pen.

"Did you need to study?" she asked, glancing at his book bag.

"Yeah, but it can wait. I need to ask you something."

"What is it?"

"Would you like to go out with me tomorrow night?" Jemma looked at him, mesmerized by his green eyes. *He's so darn sexy!*

"Yes, I'd love that."

"Good. Are you free at seven?" She nodded at his question.

"Yes. My last class is at 5:30. Where are we going?"

"I know a nice Italian restaurant we can go to," Will replied, focusing completely on her while they spoke.

"Great. I love Italian food."

He took a deep breath before continuing. "Hey, Jemma, we need to talk about—"

His words were cut off when all the lights flickered on and off in the library. The students lightly protested, the darkness from outside making the place creepy.

"Students, we have a power outage, and we need to leave the building. Please exit through the front doors in an orderly fashion," the head librarian said in a loud voice.

He waited as Jemma gathered her stuff so he could escort her out as some students from the upper floors came down to leave. Will looked around to make sure no one was paying them any attention. He grabbed Jemma's hand, and they rushed between two bookcases to the back wall where it was empty.

"Will, what—"

"The kiss. I want another one," he said, pressing her up against the wall of books and lowered his head.

Jemma didn't want to seem brazen, but she eagerly met his lips, her fingers tracing the muscles in his arms. Just like before, it was slow yet hungry. The dimness of the room added to the mood of the kiss, making it more sensual. She moaned in her throat, reaching up to stroke his face. She didn't want it to end, and her body prickled in a good way. They heard the last call from the librarian, and they pulled apart from one another to leave the building with their hands clasped.

"WHAT ARE you wearing on your date?" Sonya asked, sitting crossed legged on Jemma's bed. She had showered and was now standing in front of her closet with a towel wrapped around her body. The TV was showing an episode of *The A-Team* and the heat was on at a comfortable temperature.

"I don't know. It's too cold for a dress or skirt," Jemma replied, sliding the hangers in her closet one at a time to look at her clothes.

"How about your black slacks with my peach silk blouse? You can wear those cute strappy heels." Jemma liked the idea, heading toward her underwear drawer.

Twenty minutes later, she was dressed, with Sonya nodding her approval. "Now, have fun and flirt with him. He's super cute," Sonya said, picking a piece of lint off Jemma's shirt.

Jemma added pearl jewelry to complete her outfit and had her hair in a French roll. "Oh, shush. What are you going to do tonight?"

"Maybe go to that movie night they're having in the student lounge."

"Sounds fun."

"Not as fun as going on a date with an insanely handsome, rich guy."

"That's not why I'm going out with him, Sonya."

"I know, but you two do look cute together," Sonya said as she went to go answer the knock at the door.

Will was standing on the other side in gray slacks, a navy blazer over a blue button-down Oxford shirt, with his low-top fade freshly lined and cut, and he was holding a bouquet of lush pink carnations with baby's breath mixed in.

"Thank you, Will. They're beautiful," she said as he handed them to her.

"You're welcome."

He watched her put the flowers on a table and grab her jacket along with a purse. She turned to wave at Sonya, who waved back. The rain had long since stopped, but there was a chilliness in the air.

"You look amazing, Jemma," Will mentioned as they walked toward his black Jaguar after leaving the dorm. She blushed at his words, and he looked delighted.

"Thank you. You're looking dapper yourself."

"Thanks. You're not used to compliments, are you?"

"I'm not *not* used to them. It's just been a while since I've gotten them from the opposite sex." He held the car door open for her, and he rushed to the other side once she was settled in, the car still warm from the drive over. Jemma had to admit that riding in a luxury car was nice. It was a smooth ride, and the seats were pleasantly soft.

"I like your hair like that."

"Thanks. So, what's the name of the restaurant we're going to?"

"It's called Giuseppe's."

She quietly listened to the jazz music that was playing on the radio and watched the city streets pass by, not seeing too many people outside, and noted that Will was a safe driver. He didn't speed and came to complete stops when needed. Jemma glanced at him, studying his profile. *He is such a masculine Alpha male*, she thought. She knew there was an attraction between them, and she was curious as to where it would lead.

A few minutes later, they were parking at the restaurant, and Will escorted her inside the stylish place. It was a decent sized eatery with tables with a few booths. It had a dark Mahogany wooden floor with matching walls and modern paintings on the walls. The tables had Ivory tablecloths with the utensils sparking in the candlelight. The whole place smelled divine from tasty smells that wafted through the air.

"This is nice, Will," she said, looking around the warm atmosphere.

"I thought you'd like it," he replied as they were shown a table by the maître' d. "Order anything you want off the menu," Will told her as they were seated by the wall, a big window between Will's chair and the table behind them.

"Well, in that case, I'll have an appetizer, main course, and two desserts to go," Jemma said as her eyes roamed over the menu, a grin hidden behind it.

Will was quiet as he looked at her, his eyebrows up in surprise. "That's a lot for a little woman."

"I was just kidding, Will."

"Whew! 'Cause I was about to say…" She giggled at that, and he smiled at the sound.

"Would you join me for a glass of non-alcoholic sangria?" Will asked her, placing his menu down.

"They have that here?" Jemma asked him, and he nodded. "Well, in that case, yes."

"Good, seeing it's a special occasion and all," he mentioned as the waiter came over to their table.

"Good evening. My name is Christopher. May I take your order?"

"Ladies first." Will motioned for her to proceed, watching her interact with the waiter.

"I'll have the meat Ravioli with a side salad, no dressing."

"I'll take the individual portion of the lasagna, and I'll have the salad as well with French dressing. We'll also have a glass of the non-alcoholic sangria."

After taking their order, Christopher walked off, and Jemma looked at Will. "Why is it a special occasion, Will?"

"It's our first date, that's why."

"Ah! I see. Thank you for bringing me here."

"You're welcome. You should tell Stan so he can bring your aunt."

"I'll do that. She'd love it here." They were quiet for a few minutes as she looked around, glancing at the other patrons. The rain had started up again. The hard pounding could be heard from inside the building.

"So, how did you hear about this place?"

"My brother and friend sometimes bring their dates here, and they're always talking about how good it is," he recalled, giving her his undivided attention.

"Am I the first girl you've bought here?" she asked with an amused look on her face.

"Yes. I like to take the girls I date to different places. It doesn't make the date memorable if I take different girls to the same restaurant. Don't get me wrong, though, I'm not dating multiple women now."

She smiled at that last part, sitting back when the waiter brought their drinks. "Here's to our first date," Will said as their glasses were clinked together.

"You didn't have to say that, Will, that you're not seeing anyone right now," she pointed out as she ran her finger around the top of the glass, liking the taste of the cool drink after taking a sip.

"I don't have anything to hide. However, you are wrong about something; I am seeing you."

"This is our first date, Will."

"True. But you have to admit there's an attraction between us." She didn't say anything when Christopher bought out the salad and they thanked him.

"I'll admit it, yes. But it's more than that. When you touch me, look at me... I get this sizzling awareness inside me. This has never happened to me before, Will."

"I agree, Jemma. I feel like this thing between us... we should at least explore it. Besides, I do want to see you again."

Before she could respond, the waiter bought their dinner and two goblets of water to the table. After seeing to their needs, he left them to enjoy the food.

"I would like to see you again, Will." They ate their meal with general conversation, the rain sounds increasing outside.

"At the diner, you said you wanted to ask me out last semester, so why didn't you?" Jemma asked, glad she had remembered to ask him.

"I only saw you while you were working, and there never seemed to be a good time to have a conversation because you were so busy. So, I bided my time, and here we are. How's your food?" He threw in the question after answering her, and it made her head spin in a good way.

"It's great. Yours?"

"It's good. Have you thought about life after college?" Jemma shrugged at his question.

"With two more years to go, I haven't put much thought into it. But I do think I want to move back to Chicago."

Will looked at her with surprise. "Back to Chicago?"

"Yes. I was born and lived there until my parents were killed. My aunt moved me to D.C. because she was living here at the time."

"Have you been back since the accident?"

"No. What about your plans?"

"I just want to work hard at my law degree. I'm not sure where I want to practice though. What were your parents like?" Jemma was taken off guard at his question and liked the fact that he was curious to want to know about them.

Sonya had been the only non-family member she had talked to about her parents, and that was only after Jemma felt comfortable and they had become good friends. Will waited as he watched her have an internal debate from the look on her face. He could tell she was deciding what to tell or not tell him; either way, he would be fine with what she revealed to him. He knew firsthand how to approach this situation whenever it was mentioned.

"They were... perfect together. They supplemented each other. I don't remember a time where they ever raised their voices at each other. Of course, there were spats, but they always seemed to work it out. I know that if they were still alive, they'd still be married, driving each other batty." Jemma realized that it didn't hurt to talk about her parents anymore; it was just a deep sadness.

Whenever she made an important decision, she always asked what her parents would think and if they would approve. "Did they know you wanted to be a nurse?"

"Yes. My mom was one, and she would tell me stories about her job, the people she'd met, the medical procedures she assisted with. I don't know... I guess following in her footsteps is a way to honor her memory. But I do want to do it for myself as well. It's amazing how the human body works and how all the organs function together. I remember my aunt used to say I'd turn into a zombie whenever *Quincey, M.D.* and *M*A*S*H* came on TV."

Will laughed at those words and came to the realization he wanted to sit and talk with her all night. He liked hearing her stories and the way her face lit up when she talked about being a nurse.

"What about your father?"

"Daddy was a mailman, and the people on his route loved him. They'd make him pies, cakes, some even gave him a monetary thank you during the holidays. He never took it; he always used to say people worked hard for their money and he wasn't going to take anything extra for doing his job."

"He sounds like a good man."

"He was," she countered with a serene, inward smile. Will reached across the table and gently took her hand.

"From what I can tell, I'm sure your parents are very proud of you." She nodded at what he said, blinking back the tears that were swelling in her eyes.

"Don't make me cry on our first date, Will," she told him, lightly laughing as she pressed the napkin to dab at the wetness.

"Did you like your food?" Jemma asked, wanting to put the outing back in good spirits.

"Yes. You?" he asked, pushing away the empty plate.

"I loved it; very delicious."

"You finished your food; that's good," Will stated, looking at her plate

"Why do you say that?"

"Most girls will pick at or only eat tiny bites of their food on a first date."

"I know; I just feel comfortable around you. Besides, I was nervous about our date and hadn't eaten anything all day."

"Why were you nervous?"

"Have you seen yourself? I'm not used to a handsome man like you asking me out. I thought I'd have to force a conversation with you, but I didn't."

"Sounds like you made another assumption about me again… That hurts." He poked his bottom lip out, and she laughed.

"I'm sorry, Will. It was nerves on my part; nothing to do with you."

"Split a piece of cake with me, and we'll call it even."

"OK. Just a small piece."

"Good. I'm not ready to go yet," he admitted, signaling Christopher over. Jemma looked at Will as he placed the order, liking how his shirt fit across his wide chest.

Like Will said, she wanted to explore these feelings she had toward him and wondered if it was the real thing or not. Since she had no experience in this field, she had no idea if it was tangible or not. But what was the harm of seeing where it went? She could tell Will was a guy who protected and treated his women like a precious stone; she saw that firsthand at Chit Chat's during homecoming. Jemma looked up and caught his green eyes staring at her. They didn't say anything as that unspoken connection was back and powerful as ever. They didn't have to pretend with each other, and whatever it was—passion, lust, craving, desire—had made itself known to both of them.

"Will, where did you get your green eyes from?"

"My mother. Where did you get your hazel eyes from?"

"My father and grandfather." The chocolate cake and coffee were bought out, and she took a sip of it.

"Ooh! This is good."

"They make genuine Italian coffee here," he informed her, and she took another sip, savoring the rich, hot taste.

"Open up." She lifted her head and saw him holding a piece of dessert on a fork, his green eyes burning with intensity. Without a word, Jemma leaned forward, held his hand, and wrapped her painted lips around the offering. Will was glad the tablecloth was long enough to cover his instant erection. His manhood throbbed double time when she licked the crumbs off her bottom lip. *Get a grip, man!* Will had had his fair share of girlfriends in high school, and each were different in their own way, but Jemma was different... He knew that when he first saw her, which is why he felt like a school boy with his first crush around her. Being around her, talking to her, watching her eat... it was unnerving and exotic at the same time.

"Thank you," she whispered with glowing eyes.

"You're welcome," Will cooed in a rough voice.

Jemma watched Will slowly eat the after-dinner treat, and she felt an urging to do devious things to his virile mouth, the pinkness of his tongue teasing her. She grabbed her water glass and drank the entire contents, Will looking at her with a frown.

"Are you all right?"

"Yep, just had a dry mouth. Now, it's your turn. Tell me about your parents." Will put the fork down and placed his fists on top of the table. Jemma instantly saw his shoulders tense up, but after a few minutes, she saw it leave, and he rotated his neck, the bones cracking.

"They were like your parents. In love, happy. Dad was CEO of the company, and my mom was a photographer. She used to take pictures for the local newspaper; Rob and I still have the papers with some of her photos."

"Now, that is cool!"

"Yeah. She always had a camera around her neck, and she'd spend hours in the darkroom my dad built for her."

"Sounds like he was devoted to your mom."

"He was nuts over her and she over him. I remember on some Saturdays we would just pile in the car and go for a drive. We'd sing along with Smokey Robinson and the Miracles. Mom knew she loved her some Smokey, and my dad said he would've married Gladys Knight if he hadn't met my mother."

Jemma roared with laughter at that, and he joined in with her. "They sounded awesome."

"They were, Jemma."

"It was nice you had your brother while growing up. What type of trouble did you two get into?"

Jemma listened with detail as Will recalled all the shenanigans he got into with Robert, her side hurting from laughing so hard when he told her about the prank wars that ended with Will getting a haircut like Larry from *The Three Stooges*.

"My grandfather was so pissed! Robert got a lashing so bad he couldn't sit down for two days."

"You guys are trouble together, I see." He shrugged with glee at that, glad he could impart his memories with her. None of his ex-girlfriends had been interested about getting to know that part of him, and he was glad Jemma wasn't like that.

29

"Do you want anything else?" he asked, pushing the half-eaten cake away.

"No, I'm full." Christopher brought out the check, and Will pulled out his wallet.

"Don't insult me by doing that. I asked you out," he spoke, nodding toward her purse, which she had reached for.

She placed it down and sat back, crossing her legs. "Do you always have to get your way?" she asked as the table was cleared and he'd paid the bill.

"I don't always get my way. I just go after what I want. Right now, in addition to kissing you again, I want to spend more time with you." Jemma pulled her hands back when he reached for them, clearing her throat.

"I'm not one of those girls who goes from bed to bed, Will."

"Oh, I know that. I would never force you to do anything you didn't feel comfortable with, Jemma. That's not the type of man I am. But you're my girl now, and I want to get to know you... carry your books, help you study, give you foot massages, that type of thing." Jemma smiled at his words, reaching out to take his fingers.

"I'm your girl now?"

"Damn straight."

"And what if I have any objections to it?"

"I know ways of changing your mind, but do you have any concerns?" She smiled, shaking her head.

"Good. Ready to go?"

"Yes, let me just go to the ladies' room first. Since you paid for dinner, I'll leave Christopher a tip." By the time Jemma joined Will at the front door, his car had been brought around by the valet.

Holding an umbrella, the uniformed man escorted Jemma to the car, and Will rushed to the driver's side. He had rain dripping down his face, the exposed part of his shirt soaked with the blazer.

"I can't believe it's raining this time of year," she commented as the Jaguar's wiper blades were going full speed.

"I know. It's just going to get cold in a few weeks," Will replied, using his left hand to drive.

Biting her bottom lip, she reached down and took his right hand that was resting on the gear shift. "I don't like the cold weather," she disclosed, breaking the silence in the car.

"You don't?"

"No. The snow is fine, but when it's freezing temperatures, I can't stand it."

"You must be the type that likes to sit in front of a big fire with a cup of cocoa," he said, and she laughed.

"Something like that. You should try my cocoa. I toast marshmallows with whipped cream and chocolate shavings."

"That sounds yummy." Will parked his car in the lot across from Jemma's dorm.

"You don't mind waiting until the rain eases up, do you?" he asked, turning the car off with the radio still playing.

"No, it's fine." They were silent as the rain and easy listening music filled the car with different sounds.

"You like jazz?" Jemma asked, unbuckling the seat belt and turning toward him.

"I do, but I like other types of music as well. R&B, old school, Hip Hop."

"Me too. I like movie soundtracks, though."

"What type of movies do you like?" Will asked, undoing his seat belt as well.

"Action, comedies, horror."

"Oh, you like to be scared, huh?" Jemma chuckled. "Yes, I'd go see a scary movie, but I'm the biggest chicken around."

"Have you ever seen the movie *Halloween*?"

"No."

"You never saw- Oh, it's Halloween next week. We're going to pop some corn and watch it," he declared matter-of-factly.

Jemma didn't say anything but replied with a smile. Will picked her hand up and kissed the back of it, goosebumps appearing on her skin.

"Your hands are so soft, and they smell good."

"Thank you," she murmured.

Without saying another word, Will leaned over and connected his lips to hers. She sighed with elation as they settled into the kiss. It wasn't urgent like the one in the library, but it was just as good. They took it slow as tongues and lips caressed the other person's. Between the stroking, gentle bites, and suckling, Will became highly aroused by the simple kiss. He saw she was in the same state by her nipples pressing against the blouse, and he grinned to himself when she let out a shaky breath. Even after the rain had let up, the duo wasn't in any rush to leave the car since they both wanted the kiss to keep going, and it indeed went on for a long time.

CHAPTER 3

It was the day of the debate meeting, and Jemma was looking down at her notes, looking over key points she had written down. She was sitting next to a short girl named Thomasina as the auditorium filled with people to watch the discussion, and the opposing school had brought a fair share of their students for moral support. The room was circular in shape with the seats that led to an incline. The seats were cushioned and a tan color, the curtains were separated into two parts, and they were a velvet mustard colored cloth. Foldup tables had been set up for the teams that held a pitcher of water with disposable cups.

The third member of the team, Felicia Childress, joined them on stage, and Jemma rolled her eyes. She didn't like Felicia... plain and simple. She was a light-skinned girl with a high fashioned hair style and always wore designer clothes. She was a spoiled daddy's girl who believed she didn't have to work hard at anything. She'd only joined the debate team because her dad said it'd look good on her academic record. She barely came to the meetings, but the coach excused her a lot because of the contributions her parents made to the school.

"It sure is a lot of cute guys from St. Trinity here," Felicia said with a sly grin. They were wearing their debate uniforms of khaki pants and a white button down with the school crest over the pocket.

"We're not here to look at boys, Felicia. If we win today, we can leave the semester undefeated," Thomasina said, and Felicia shrugged.

"So what? After this, I'm leaving the team anyway."

"Good," Jemma replied, and Felicia rolled her eyes at her. Once the debate got underway and the topic of women in politics was introduced, Howard won the coin toss to go first. Just as Jemma was about to speak, Will walked into the auditorium, closing the door behind him, and Jemma watched as he sat in the empty aisle seat in the fourth row.

"Oh my God! What is William Rutherford doing here?" Felicia gasped under her breath, and Jemma heard her.

"Miss Alden, please respond," the mediator said, and Will winked at her before she answered. After an hour, Howard ended up winning the debate by a landslide even though they had a teammate whose contribution was the bare minimum.

While she was gathering her things, Jemma watched Felicia approach Will, noticing she had flipped her hair and added an extra switch to her hips.

"Excuse me, I'm Felicia Childress. I know your grandmother, Mona. She's on the same fundraiser committee with my mother, Georgina." Will looked at her for a second before trying to move past her, but she blocked his path. "Good to know. Excuse me, please."

"Now, why are you in such a hurry, William?" She had lowered her voice to sound sexy, but it came out nasally, and Will tried not to roll his eyes.

"It's none of your business, Miss. Childress." He moved past her, and Felicia saw him walk toward Jemma, both people smiling. Felicia stormed out in a jealous fit, determined to find out the nature of their relationship way. William Rutherford belonged with Felicia Childress, not with a person like Jemma Alden. Will continued to praise Jemma's debating skills as he took her to her dorm so she could change clothes. It was Halloween night, and some people were walking around in costumes or Halloween-themed clothing. The movie night was to be held at his apartment, and she was a little anxious since this would be the first time meeting his brother and best friend. When Sonya walked in minutes later with her book bag, she saw Will sitting on the couch and nodded at him.

"Hey, Will. Where's Jemma?"

"Hello, Sonya. She went to change her clothes. How are you?"

"I'm good. I just got stood up, but I'm good."

"I'm sorry. You want me to go kick his ass?" he asked, and she chuckled.

"No, it's OK. I'll just stay here and study, I guess." Sonya sighed at that last part, blowing out a deep breath.

"C'mon. It's Friday night and it's Halloween. We're having a movie night at my place, and you're more than welcome to join us. We have pizza, popcorn and drinks." Jemma was standing in the hallway, listening to Will invite Sonya over to his place so she wouldn't be alone tonight. *He's so generous*, she thought.

"No, I don't want to be a third wheel for your date."

"You won't be. My brother and other roommate will be there too. We're just going to watch movies and hang out," Will informed her.

"If it's OK with Jemma, I'll go," Sonya tossed over her shoulder as she walked out the room.

Jemma met her in the hall and nodded with a smile before Sonya could ask. Jemma went to where Will was standing, stood on her tiptoes, and gave him a slow kiss.

"Thanks for inviting Sonya."

"You're welcome, babe. You keep thanking me like that, and she can come with us all the time," Will said, and she let out a loud titter.

She had changed into a white sweater and jeans, and as soon as Sonya re-entered the room, the trio left to go enjoy their night. Turns out since Will had his Roadster, they had to ride to his apartment with Jemma sitting on Sonya's lap. Will's place was on the second floor, and it had three bedrooms with two bathrooms. It had carpeted floors with a small kitchen and a big dining/living room combo. White walls had a gray trim which were decorated with art pieces and pictures.

"Geez! Who decorated your place, Will?" Sonya asked, sitting on the black leather L-shaped sectional with a matching coffee table and entertainment center.

"My grandparents paid extra to have the place decorated." On the dining room table was a big bowl of ice with soft drinks and bottles of water in it. Robert and Brandon had walked in a few seconds later carrying two boxes of large pizzas and a bag of videos as Will introduced the four people.

"Excuse me, ladies." Will left the room, and the four people got pedigree info from one another.

Robert and Will favored each other by having the same physique and height. Robert's fade was higher than Will's, and he hugged Jemma, glad to put a face to the name. The girls had made small talk with Robert, while Brandon went to go make popcorn in the kitchen. Jemma smiled as Robert was telling funny anecdotes about his brother. Sonya got up to see the movies that were placed on the VCR, and Robert went to gather paper plates and napkins.

"What do they have?"

"*Halloween, Halloween 2*, and *Sleepaway Camp*. Have you seen any of these?"

"No. You?"

"Nope."

"That's good, Sonya. If you get scared, I'll protect you from the boogeyman." She swung toward Brandon with her hands on her hips. He had a big container of butter popcorn, and she frowned at him. Brandon was tall like his roommates, had a mustard colored complexion, and he had designs cut into the back of his head. He had dark brown eyes and an average looking face.

"That's OK. I don't need your protection," Sonya let him know, and he smirked at her.

Will walked back into the room with a plain white undershirt and gray sweat pants on with white socks. The group watched the movies and ate the food with fright and funny commentary. Afterwards, a game of Clue got underway, and they all were entertained because each selection he'd made, Robert ended up being the culprit. It was almost 3 a.m. when they signed into the front desk to get back into their dorm room, Jemma admitting that this was the best Halloween she had had in a long time.

∽

The first half of sophomore year was slowly coming to an end. It was Thanksgiving break, and the couple had parted ways as Will went to his grandparents and Jemma went home. Of course, Stan was there, and Sonya decided to stay with them during the holiday. Since the students only had three days off for the break, her best friend saw no reason to fly home then have to fly right back to school from Atlanta, so she was going to stay in the guest bedroom at Aunt Paris's. The guardian didn't mind the extra company; she liked Sonya and knew she was a good girl and a great friend to her niece.

Across town, Will, Robert, and Brandon were in the family room of the former's grandparents' mansion waiting on the older couple to make an appearance. The house was filled with the smells of a roasting turkey, dressing, and other goodies. The mansion was a Tudor style home with dark colored brinks and a tiled roof. The foyer was a wide, open space with polished slate gray tile. A wide, carpeted staircase led up to the second floor where an oil painting of flowers rested on the wall next to a top curved window. The first floor held the family room that had windows on two walls, marble pillars, and a baby grand piano. The furniture was expensive and well-maintained with a fireplace that wasn't being utilized. The rest of the lower interior had a TV room, dining room, and office with bookshelves along the walls. There were seven bedrooms total with an attached powder room, with the basement and attic being used for storage.

"Are you serious, man?" Will looked at his younger brother, who had just announced that, he was going to sign up for the Marines after college.

"Yes. I need a challenge, a sense of purpose. Joining the military will help with that especially since I don't have a major yet."

"You know your grandmother is going to have a shit fit," Brandon said, drinking the last of his water.

"I know, but it's my life. She has no choice but to accept it."

"Accept what?" Mona Rutherford had come in on the tail end of the conversation, decked out in a forest-green designer pantsuit with pearls at her throat and ears, her hair in a neat chignon.

At fifty-two and five feet four, she might have appeared to be a tiny woman, but she had spunk and could hold her own. She liked for things to go her way, and because she was fair skinned with money, she thought she had the upper hand with black folks who had less than she did. Even though her only child had disobeyed her wishes and married a girl she didn't approve of, Mona did love her grandsons and would see to it that they married well within their class.

"Hello, Grandmother," Will said, giving her a kiss on her cheek.

"Thank you for letting me stay for the break, Mrs. Rutherford," Brandon said, and she smiled at him.

"You're welcome, dear. Now, what will I have to accept, Robert?"

The two guys stepped back, and he gave them the evil eye. *Chickens!* "I'm auditioning for the lead in the school play *Cat on a Hot Tin Roof*," Robert said instead, and Will bit back a laugh.

"Honestly, Robert, what are you going to do with an acting degree?"

Joshua Rutherford walked in at his wife's words donning an ivory turtleneck with navy trousers. At six feet two, he towered over his wife, and they could not be more different. Joshua was a bald, cocoa skin gentleman with gentle eyes and a slim figure. He was quiet and introverted, unlike Mona. Will always wondered at the nature of their relationship. He never saw them smile at each other or have a decent conversation; to him, it appeared as though they simply tolerated each other.

"That's one of my favorite Tennessee Williams' plays; you'd make a great Brick," Joshua said, and the younger man smiled.

"Thank you, Granddad," Robert replied.

A few minutes later, they were seated in the grand dining room with two huge chandeliers. The walls were white, and over the stone fireplace, the wall had cherub etchings carved into it. The windows had fancy, patterned curtains that were open, and the table had two big flowered centerpieces in the middle. A mushroom colored plush Italian rug was on the floor to complement the art hanging on the wall. The cook had outdone herself with the traditional feast including rice and apricot dressing and homemade cranberry sauce.

"It's so nice to see my boys home at the same time even though Howard isn't that far away. I still don't get to see you a lot." Mona began the conversation after Joshua had carved the turkey.

"They're busy being college students, Mona. Surely you remember those good times," Joshua retorted, sipping his wine, and she snorted.

"Good times for whom?" she asked under her breath, but the three guys had heard her, Brandon clearing his throat at the awkward moment.

"Well, you know, we're just studying, keeping busy," Will replied to her.

"Speaking of which, I saw Georgina Childress and her daughter Felicia at the country club yesterday. Felicia told me you came to her debate meeting. She's a nice girl, Will. She comes from a very connected family," Mona told him, and he ate the food on his fork, wondering where that statement came from.

"She might be nice, but she lied to you. I didn't go to see her. I went to support Jemma."

His grandparents looked up at his words, Joshua shocked because he didn't know Will was seeing anyone, Mona fuming due to the fact she didn't know this faceless girl.

"Who is this young lady, Will?" the patriarch asked, eating some mashed potatoes.

"Jemma Alden. She's a sophomore and a nursing major. We've been seeing each other for a few weeks now," Will responded to his grandfather's question.

"Alden... Alden... I don't believe I know that name," Mona said, cutting into the meat with the silver cutlery.

"Who cares about her name, Grams?"

"Well, it's going to matter because the Rutherford's have to keep our name linked to those who have prestige and notability. We come from one of the oldest families in the county, and we must maintain that creed. I don't know the Alden name, which means she doesn't come from our circle."

Here she goes with this nobility crap again, Will said to himself, rolling his eyes.

Robert could feel the irritation seething off his older brother from across the big oak table, and he decided to interject.

"Now, Will, just let her—"

He stopped talking from the look Will gave him, deciding to let them hash it out.

"Grams, I don't know how many times I have to tell you I am not interested in dating someone from *your circle*. I don't care about that; you do. I like Jemma and she likes me. Why is that such an issue?" Will asked, and they were eyeballing each other.

"I swear, William, you sound just like—"

"Like who?"

"Your father. Whenever he talked about that green-eyed—"

Will sprang out his chair and stormed over to her, where he pulled the seat back and pointed his finger at her.

"You better think carefully about your next words toward my mother!"

"Hey, Will. C'mon, man." Robert and Brandon had both stood up, the latter saying the words to calm down his friend.

Will looked at his grandmother again before leaving the room. Seconds later, the front door slammed shut, and Robert gave Mona a disgusted look before leaving the room with Brandon following him.

"Aren't you going to say something, Joshua?" Mona asked as her husband took a deep breath.

"No. You're the only one who's obsessed with preserving the family name. Our grandsons have turned into fine men, and I will back them up with everything I have. I won't let you pawn them off on just anyone and they end up miserable like we are now."

With that, Joshua left the table as well, leaving Mona to herself. She continued eating, a just-in-case plan forming in her head. She wouldn't use it unless Will insisted on continuing seeing that Jemma Alden girl.

She wouldn't let Robert and Will do what their father had done. He had defied Mona and married Rachel Youngman anyway, a girl he loved, but Mona knew she wasn't right for him. Rachel had come from a meager family who wasn't well-versed on things like fine art and politics. Rachel simply wasn't good enough, in Mona's opinion, and she would do whatever it took for her grandson to not make the same mistake.

∼

"You know, I think you women folk are conspiring against me to take all my money," Stan said as he paid Sonya one hundred dollars after he landed on her property, causing Jemma and Paris to laugh.

They had finished Thanksgiving dinner and were almost done with their game of Monopoly.

"Sorry, Uncle Stan."

"Uh huh." Sonya chuckled just as the doorbell rang, and Paris went to answer it.

"That's OK. I'm planning my comeback." Jemma smiled as Paris walked back into the dining room.

"Jemma, Will is here." She got up from the table, left the room, and saw him standing in the hallway with his jacket undone.

"Hi, Will."

"Hey, babe." They embraced each other, and she noticed that he had hugged her tighter than usual.

"Are you OK?" He nodded, and she searched his eyes. "I don't believe you," she stated, and he let out a small smile that didn't reach his eyes.

"I didn't mean to disrupt your dinner."

"We're finished eating and playing a board game. You're not fine, Will. Let's go into the kitchen."

She took his hand, and they headed toward the warm room at the back of the two-story house. The kitchen was small and cozy with cream cabinets and black appliances. Splashes of color were sprinkled around the room from the yellow flour holder to the red oven mitts.

Paris had come into the kitchen and was fiddling around in the junk drawer.

"Is the game over?"

"Yes. We cleaned Stan out. The movie is coming on in a few minutes."

"Thanks, Auntie." Will and Jemma sat at the square chrome table, and he slung his coat over the back of the chair.

"I'm happy to see you, Will," Jemma stated, their hands interlocking.

"Me too. I didn't know where else to go, and I didn't want to go back to my empty apartment."

"You want to talk about what happened?"

He told her about the words exchanged with his grandmother, and Jemma sat there shocked. "Oh, wow."

"I just don't understand her sometimes."

She could see the anguish on his face about what happened at dinner. He hated being at odds with Mona, but she had to understand he and Robert weren't like her. They weren't uppity and thought they were better than the next person just because they grew up with money.

"Did she not like your mother at all?" Jemma asked with disbelief. How could Will's grandmother not like his mother with a valid, tangible reason?

"No. All because she wasn't born in the 'right family'. My parents adored each other deeply, and they loved us. That's the only thing that counts."

"I agree." Will smiled at her, and she heard his stomach growl.

"You haven't eaten?"

"We had just sat down to dinner when we argued, and I left," he replied.

"Boy!" she exclaimed, sucking on her teeth. She stood up and went to the fridge and began to take out the leftovers.

"What are you doing?"

"Fixing you a plate. Your stomach sounds like a grizzly bear."

"You don't have to—"

"Shush."

"But that's for—"

"Shush."

"Ain't gon' be too many shushes..." he mumbled, and she smiled softly as she warmed up a big plate of food. Stan came into the kitchen and started to make a pot of coffee.

"Everything good, son?"

"Yes, sir. Sorry for barging in like this."

"It's not a problem; the more the merrier. It's plenty of food if you want some more."

"Uncle Stan, is the movie on yet?"

"It's on right now."

"What movie is that?" Will asked.

"*Jaws*. We've never seen it."

"You've never seen *Jaws*? What is it with this family not seeing classic films?"

"That's what I said, Will. C'mon, you two," Stan said, carrying two cups of coffee.

After the movie ended, Sonya said goodnight as she made her way upstairs to the spare bedroom to call her parents. After cleaning the kitchen and starting the dishwasher, Paris placed a pillow with a blanket and sheet on the couch.

"This is in case you don't want to drive home, you can sleep down here," she said to Will, and he nodded.

"Thank you."

"You're welcome." Stan followed her upstairs, leaving the two youngsters alone in the living room.

They were sitting on the Periwinkle two-seater couch with the TV and lights off, the only light coming from the fireplace which had two big pieces of wood burning in it. Jemma had on blue jeans and a yellow low-cut sweater with matching socks.

"Did you like *Jaws*?" Will had his arm wrapped around her shoulders, and she snuggled against his side. His loafers were off, and his feet were crossed at the ankles.

"You mean the world's biggest shark? Yes, I liked it."

"I'm making it my mission to get you to look at all the classic movies," he told her, and she grinned, draping one arm across his stomach.

"Are you nervous about finals coming up?" she asked after they were quiet for a few minutes.

"No. You?"

"Nope. I'm passing my classes, so I'm good."

"That's 'cause you're a smart woman," he mumbled against her forehead. "Just so you know, I'm getting you something for Christmas." Jemma sat up and turned to look at him.

"You don't have to buy me anything, Will," she said in a low voice, and the look he gave her made her want to take back her words.

"I'm going to ignore what you just said, Jemma. I won't be here at that time, and I want you to have something to open from me." She bit her lip, and he looked at her full bottom one, reaching out to cup her cheeks.

"I'll have something for you as well."

"If that's what you want to do, that's fine by me."

Will pulled her toward him to sit on top of his lap sideways, and she bent down to kiss him. She cupped his face between warm hands as their tongues slowly mated. It was unhurried, deep, and relaxed. She could still taste the sweetness from the dessert on his tongue, Will's hands spanning her waist to keep her in place. They were enjoying smooching one another so much... Jemma was doing this thing with her tongue to stroke his that drove Will mad! He moved down to cup and squeeze her ass, and her breath hitched.

"I knew your butt would feel nice and plump," he whispered against her lips, giving a solid caress.

She let out a nervous giggle, her breath coming out in unsteady gasps. "You OK, baby?"

"Yes."

"Do you want me to stop touching you?"

"Oh, no! Don't stop doing that." Will saw her nipples pressing against her sweater, and he wondered if she could feel the massive hard-on she was sitting on.

"Will..." She shifted on him and he groaned.

"Are you... Is that your—?"

"Yes."

"Oh!"

She had felt him swell up and knew why she suddenly felt a tingling achiness between her legs. It felt like an iron rod under her buttocks, and she kind of did a little butt jiggle on him, causing him to grimace in pain and pleasure. Will took her right hand and slid it between their bodies. He thought Jemma's eyes would pop out her head when she touched him with a timid stroke, feeling his stiffness through his trousers. She watched Will's head fall back on the couch with his eyes closed as he enjoyed the contact. As she got used to fondling his thickness, her touch became more gratifying and lost its initial hesitation.

"You're the first guy I've touched like this," she confessed to him in a small voice.

"And I'll be the last too."

"Does it hurt?" she asked, pressing her chest against his with her hand still moving up and down on him.

"It hurts in a good way, baby. For a virgin, you positively are trying to seduce me."

She looked at him, surprised at his words. How had he known? Was it the way she was acting, or was it the bashfulness she'd expressed to him a few times? "You know I'm a virgin?"

"Yes, which is good because I can show you all the great things about making love whenever you're ready."

Hmmm... what things? His words caused her to stop her fondling, and she rested her hands on his shoulders.

"You're willing to wait, Will?"

"As long as it takes, honey. I'm damn sure not going to rush you, and I want you to be 100 percent ready before taking that step."

"You're so sweet to me," she told him softly, and he grinned at her. Jemma knew she could trust and believe Will's words. She knew he wouldn't force her to do anything she wasn't comfortable with, and it was at that moment that she was sure she'd give her virginity to Will... whenever the time was right, and she was prepared.

"Now, I'm only a flesh and blood man, Jemma. If I cop a feel every now and then, you'd have to excuse me," he grumbled, and she let out a deep chuckle.

"You can get a feel now, if you want," she told him, feeling the heated flush of desire wash over her, causing her voice to deepen into a sexy growl. He reached around to squeeze her behind, and she moaned softly. She grabbed his hands and brought them to her breasts.

"I meant here." He took no time gently caressing and rubbing the heavy mounds. As he ran his thumbs repeatedly over her nipples, she leaned forward and placed her lips on his. Jemma wrapped her arms around his head as she was consumed by this new feeling Will had awoken in her... hunger. She didn't mind his hands roaming all over her body as she reached under his shirt to feel his hot chest, the young couple continuing the heavy necking on the couch late into the night.

∼

DURING A COLD DECEMBER MONTH, the last few weeks of school were coming to an end. Once Thanksgiving was over, most of the students went on finals lockdown. The library and computer labs had extended their hours to accommodate the finals schedule. Will and Jemma were excited because they had signed up for classes related to their majors for next year. Will and his roommates ended up having many study sessions at their apartment for some of their classmates that included Jemma and Sonya. Will and his family headed to Aspen for their annual Christmas vacation a few days after school ended, and Sonya flew home to Atlanta.

Jemma was excited to go home for the holiday because Paris and Stan always decorated the house with festive trimmings. Even though she stayed on campus, her aunt still had her bedroom waiting for her at whenever she needed it. The day before school let out, Jemma and Will had gotten together to exchange gifts with each person giving two presents a piece. Will was standing against the wall-length window, looking at the snow-capped mountains. After arriving by plane a few hours ago, Brandon and Robert had hit the slopes as soon as they unpacked their suitcases. Will had promised he would join them at the ski lodge for hot drinks in an hour. The cabin was located a few miles from the main road, not far from the very popular Emerald Pines Ski Resort.

It had wide French doors that opened up to a circular parlor with a fireplace. A very spacious living and dining room was on the first floor with a kitchen that ran the width of the house. Upstairs, his grandparents shared the master bedroom, but the house had nine other bedrooms with separate bathrooms. Will would get out and ski eventually; he just missed Jemma…a lot. He was anxious to see the presents she'd gotten for him, but they had made a deal with each other to not open them until Christmas, which was two days away. He didn't know the extent of his feelings for Jemma yet, but he knew it was driving him crazy to not see her every day. He was already missing her smile, her eyes, the way her hips swayed when she walked, the dimples in her cheek…

Letting out a deep breath, he glanced toward the tall, stylish Christmas tree on the opposite wall with expensive ornaments and an abundance of multicolored presents under it and wondered what his grandparents were up to. The last time he saw Joshua he was in the library on a conference call, and Mona had the help getting the guest bedrooms ready. His grandmother always invited one of her country club friends and their family to spend the holiday with them. Will thought it was so she could show the place off, but one never knew with Mona.

"Oh, Will, good. You're here. I want you to greet my guests with me. They should be here in a minute, and your grandfather is unavailable."

"Sure Grams," he replied just as the doorbell rang. He joined her in the foyer as the butler headed toward the door. Will looked on with annoyance and vexation as Felicia Childress walked in with her parents.

WILL STOOD under the warm water in the shower, letting it melt away the day's dirt and stress. After going to the lodge to vent to his brother and Brandon about the houseguests, they stayed in the ski lounge until it closed at ten o'clock. When they got back, everyone was sitting in the living room having drinks in front of the fireplace and talking. Felicia had invited Will to sit next to her, but he declined and sat next to Joshua. He told Jemma he would call her later that night, and that was his next move after he got out the shower. Drying off and throwing on brown flannel pajama pants, he was walking toward the bed when he heard a knock on the door. Felicia was standing at the door wearing a fluffy robe that was loosely tied, giving anyone a view of her small breast.

"Are you kidding me?" Will asked, leaning against the door.

"I'm here to give you your Christmas present," she stated in a whiney drone.

"I don't want anything from you. You might want to cover yourself up." Felicia noticed that Will hadn't looked at her exposed skin, and that made her more determined.

She knew once she did her thing on his impressive package, he wouldn't be talking that way. Per several male associates, she had a gifted mouth, which she used to get things to go her way at one point or another. Once she got on her knees and did what she did best, he would change his tune.

"You don't want me to leave. Do you, Will?"

"Yes, I do. I need to make an important call." He was about to close the door when she blocked it with her hand.

"I would love it if you could teach me how to ski tomorrow."

"Brandon is the better skier. Ask him. Goodnight." He closed and locked the door before walking over to the queen size bed.

He usually wasn't rude to women, but Felicia kept throwing herself at him, and he didn't know any other way to tell her he wasn't interested. Will lay across the bed and reached for the phone, anxious to hear his beautiful and classy girlfriend's voice.

In her room, Felicia was pacing with her hands on her hips. *How dare Will refuse her!* She was Felicia Childress, and they would be perfect together. She knew it, and Will's grandmother knew it. She honestly didn't see what he saw in that dowdy Jemma Alden. She wasn't rich, her family wasn't illustrious, and she didn't have the same high-end style as Felicia. She let out a deep breath and tried to think of a plan to get into Will's pants and heart.

∼

JEMMA WAS LYING in the bed on her stomach reading a book. Her legs were bent at the knees, and she was slowly moving them back and forth. The TV was showing *A Christmas Story* , but she wasn't watching it. There was a cup of her famous hot chocolate with a plate of gingerbread cookies that her aunt had baked sitting on the bedside table. A single lamp on the other table was on, casting a soft glow in the room. She wore a purple and white nightshirt that stopped at the middle of her thighs. The blare of the phone ringing caused her to jump, and she picked it up.

"Hello?"

"Hey, babe." Jemma smiled and sat up, flipping the book over.

"Hi, Will. How are you? How's Aspen?"

"I'm good, missing you like crazy. Aspen is OK. How are you?"

"I'm fine. It's been snowing a lot here. The news said we're supposed to get six inches."

"Good snowball weather." She chuckled and pulled her knees up.

"How was your day?" he asked.

"It was nice. The Christmas program was at the church tonight, and we went caroling afterwards."

"That's cool. I didn't think people still did that."

"We only went to a few blocks due to the cold and snow."

"I bet. What are you doing tomorrow?"

"Absolutely nothing, and I love it. What about you?" she asked, twirling the phone cord.

"The three of us will probably hit the slopes, but we're going to volunteer at the soup kitchen in the morning."

"That's a nice thing to do." He smiled at that and cleared his throat.

"I have to tell you something, though," he said as she took a sip of her hot drink.

"What's wrong?"

"My grandmother always invites some of her country club friends to come up during the holiday, and this year, she invited the Childresses"

"As in…"

"Yes. Felicia and her parents."

"Felicia is there with you?"

"She's here with her parents. She's not here with me," Will corrected her, and she was quiet as she processed the news.

She knew she didn't have to worry about anything on Will's part, but Felicia was another story; she was a shady little thing.

"Jemma, you there?"

"Yes, I'm here."

"You got silent on me."

"I was just thinking about what you said. She wants you in any shape or form. The fact that she's there in tight quarters… she's likely to try any trick in the book to get you," Jemma told him, adjusting the pillows behind her back.

Will turned on his side in the bed and looked at the snow-covered mountains from the window across from the bed.

"She can try anything she wants. She doesn't appeal to me at all and I'm not interested. I'm with the girl I want to be with. Don't forget that."

Jemma smiled at his words. He was so sweet and reassuring, and she liked that about him.

"I do have an important question, Jemma. What do you have on?" She smiled, knowing they would be on the phone for a long time.

CHAPTER 4

The year 1984 had entered its year-long stay with lots of snow and cold weather. The New Year celebration had kicked off without any problems, and those who had observed it hoped it would be a good, productive year. Jemma had finished wiping down everything in the dorm room and had cracked the window to let in the cold air. She was glad to be back on campus and was looking forward to taking nursing classes in addition to spending more time with Will. She had gotten back to school two days ago and he had gotten back yesterday. The spring semester was to start in four days, and Sonya was scheduled to be back early Saturday morning. Will had called and asked Jemma to come over to his apartment once she got settled, and she agreed after they had a ten-minute discussion about him coming to pick her up. Jemma convinced him she was fine with walking to his apartment since she had spent the last few weeks indoors and didn't mind the stroll to get some fresh air. It had stopped snowing, and there were piles of snow from where it had been plowed into several paths on campus.

Bundled in a lavender coat with matching hat and gloves, Jemma walked past a few students and quickened her pace to take the short cut to Will's place, anxious to see him. While he was waiting on

Jemma to show up, Will had just closed the window in the living room and turned the thermostat up a bit. The apartment needed to be aired out since it had been closed for a few weeks, and Robert and Brandon had left to get their books from the bookstore at the student center. There was a soft knock on the door, and he went to answer it. Jemma had taken her hat and gloves off as she jogged up the stairs. She didn't have to use the buzzer since someone was coming out the building as she was walking up. He opened the door, and they both smiled at each other.

"Hi, Will."

"Hey, honey."

He grabbed her by the waist to pull her inside and closed the door. Their lips eagerly met each other's in the entry. She felt nothing but pleasure and desire when their mouths connected as their tongues did a slow dance. Her hands moved from around his neck to travel down his chest and under his sweater. He had a tank top under it, and her fingers slowly ran over his scorching, solid muscles. After a few minutes, when he was satisfied with the kiss, he lifted his head and placed a kiss to her forehead.

"Hi," she said again, and he chuckled.

"You already said that. How was your break?"

"It was fine, long. Yours?"

"The same."

She had forgotten how good Will smelled. When she leaned forward and sniffed his neck, Will noticed she was wearing the diamond stud earrings he'd given to her for Christmas, and he smiled at that.

"Where are your roomies?" she asked, taking off her coat.

"They went to get their books." She nodded, and he took her hand to lead them into his bedroom and closed the door.

It was an average size room with a full-size long bed, a wooden desk that could seat two people, a TV stand that held the set and a stereo with detachable speakers. He had a dark green blanket with matching pillows on the bed and a poster of Pam Grier on his wall.

"This is a nice room. Very manly," she stated, looking around as he sat on the bed.

Jemma reached for a photo of an older smiling couple, with the woman on the man's back, and his hands tucked under her thighs. She assumed it was his parents given the eye color of the woman.

"Your mother was very pretty, and you look like your dad," she said softly, and he smiled.

"That was taken three years before they were killed."

She carefully replaced the photo and looked at him. "You don't seem nervous to be in here."

"Why would I? I know you won't hurt me."

"Got that right."

"You look tired, Will."

"I am a little bit. I have been so anxious to get back and get settled. I haven't been sleeping a lot."

"That's not good, sweetie."

"I know, but I feel better being back here with you." Jemma looked happy at his words.

"Me too, Will." He yawned, and she looked at him with kind eyes.

"It looks like you need a nap," she mentioned in a low voice.

"It wouldn't hurt. Come get in the bed with me," he insisted, standing up to take his sweater off to reveal a white tank top, and she was able to see his muscles up close. He had a nice, hard six-pack stomach that was lean with a wide chest.

"Oh, wow!" She whispered, and he grinned.

Jemma took her hoodie off, and she had on a dark blue cami' top with a matching bra. He turned the radio on with the volume low, and they got into the bed. They didn't get under the blanket, and they faced each other on the bed, each having their own pillows.

"How many classes do you have?" she asked, resting her arm against his chest as he pulled her closer with his hand draped over her hips.

"Five, and two are for my major. What about you?"

"The same, except three are for nursing."

Will ran his thumbs across the swell of her breasts, and she shuddered. She leaned forward to kiss his lips as he pulled her closer to him.

"You're making me forget about my nap," he stated after a while against her lips, and she chuckled.

"I'm sorry." She turned her back to him, and he cradled her to his chest. A few minutes later, the couple was fast asleep.

∽

Sonya was studying for her business class and eating a bowl of chili when Jemma walked in wearing her work uniform. It was a Thursday night, and light snow was falling on the ground. Jemma had changed clothes, grabbed her books, and headed toward the desk with some food. Per the housing services guidelines, residents could have an approved hot plate in the dorm, which cut back on them having to go out to get something to eat.

"Thanks for making dinner tonight."

"It's no problem. How was work?"

"Tiring. What are you studying?"

Sonya sighed with exhaustion before answering. "We have to come up with a mock business plan for a company complete with a name and projected revenue for the first year. The teacher designated the type of business, and I got a baby store."

"Have you decided on a name?"

"No. I'm bouncing ideas around in my head." Jemma thought about it as she ate some chili, opening her anatomy book.

"How about this… have a direct line for emergency services in case someone goes into labor. Offer some type of classes a few nights a week like Mommy and Me, Daddy and Me, and CPR for Babies given by nurses or midwives. You can call the store *Baby Steps*," she suggested, and Sonya gushed with delight.

"Jemma, you are a genius! Thank you!" She excitedly started writing, and her roommate grinned.

Two hours later, Jemma closed her book and yawned.

"I saw Will earlier, and he wanted to know if you wanted to go bowling with us Saturday night."

"Hmm... I don't know."

"Brandon will be there," Jemma said in a sing-song tone and Sonya sucked her teeth after rolling her eyes.

"Who cares? He thinks he's God's gift to women." Sonya replied with an attitude.

"C'mon, it'll be fun. Please, Sonya." Jemma poked out her bottom lip, and she laughed.

"OK, geez. Speaking of you and Will, have you two…"

"No! Not yet."

"OK, I was just asking. I think it's a good thing you're waiting."

"He's such a sweetheart by waiting, but it's hard cause he's such a hottie." Sonya laughed and nodded her head.

"I understand. I wish I would've waited."

"But I thought you and Doug were in love."

Sonya took a minute and thought about her high school boyfriend whom she had dated for three years. "We were; I guess it was just puppy love."

He had gotten a scholarship to the University of Texas, and they'd parted ways after graduation.

"Do you miss him?"

"Yes and no. But going back to your situation… Just in case you and Will decide to take things further, you should be prepared."

"What do you mean?"

"If your hormones do get the best of you two, you don't want to be caught wearing old bloomers and plain bras," Sonya replied to Jemma who gasped.

"My undies aren't old bloomers."

"We need to plan a trip to the mall and get you some sexy underwear—lace, silky thongs, multicolored push-up bras. He'll go nuts if he sees you wearing a cute G-string."

"You think so?" Jemma knew Will was experienced. Maybe he was the kind of guy who liked to see his girl in sexy undergarments.

"It wouldn't hurt," Sonya answered.

"OK. We can go this weekend."

"Fine by me. I'm sure my daddy wouldn't mind if I used the emergency credit card to get a few clothes." Jemma chuckled at that, shaking her head.

"Is Will your first serious boyfriend?" Sonya asked as she turned in the chair to face her friend. She was wearing a black jogging suit with house shoes on. Jemma went to go sit on her bed and put a pillow on her lap.

"I've had boyfriends in high school, but none came close to what I'm feeling for Will." Sonya went to sit next to her, the radio on in the background.

"I'm glad you aren't like some of these silly females and lose their focus once they get a guy."

"I wouldn't do that. I don't know how things will be with us in six months, but being a nurse is my top priority. So, this project you did tonight, is it a big one?"

Sonya nodded and let out a deep breath. "Yes, it's worth thirty percent of the grade. It's so cool that my professor is a woman. You don't see too many females in the marketing field."

Sonya wanted to be a marketing research analyst because she was a people person and it was second nature to her. She was good a projecting sales numbers and campaigning for profitability. "I bet it is. You're going to take the marketing world by storm," Jemma reassured her friend who cocked her head to the side.

"I hope so. I need to make sure my grades are top notch for next semester so I can try to get an internship."

"Do you know which ones will be open?"

"Not right now, no. But it would be advantageous to keep my GPA up."

"You got this, Sonya. You're one of the smartest women I know, and the good thing is, we help each other out when we can."

"Oh, I agree. You sure helped me out earlier; I was stumped. Thank you." They hugged one another, and they planned their trip to the mall.

RUTHERFORD'S WOMEN

A FEW DAYS LATER, Mona was in the sitting room looking at a few decorating magazines. She was thinking about changing the dining room around and needed some ideas. Except for the occasional pot clanging in the kitchen, the house was quiet. Joshua had left for the office hours ago, and he had done so without saying goodbye. Mona wasn't going to admit that it bothered her a little bit. Before leaving the house, he would usually give her a peck on the cheek. But lately, he stopped doing that and would barely speak to her. It was a cold day, and she was glad the fireplace was being used. The phone rang, and she leaned over to answer on the third ring.

"Hey, Grams," Will said when she picked up.

"Will, darling, how are you?"

"I'm OK. What about you and Granddad?"

"We're both well. What's with the surprise call?"

"Rob and I are coming over for Sunday dinner."

"Oh, that's great."

"I'm also bringing Jemma. I want you two to meet her."

Mona didn't say anything for a few heartbeats.

"Grams?"

"I'm here. Sure, bring her by."

Will ran down a list of things Jemma was allergic to, but she wasn't paying attention.

"OK. We'll see you all on Sunday."

She hung up and began to make a dinner menu. *Now, when was the last time we had seafood?*

～

JEMMA HAD butterflies in her stomach as Will pulled up in front of a big estate. This clearly was the rich part of town, and the neighborhood shouted it loud and proud with the huge manicured lawns and foreign cars parked in the driveways. She had on black slacks with a gold colored blouse and Mary Jane shoes. There was a chill in the air, but Will made sure the car was nice and warm for her.

"Nervous?" Will asked as he held the car door open for her.

"A little," she admitted in a small voice. He cupped her face and gently kissed her on the lips.

"Everything will be OK, babe." She smiled at him, and they headed up the steps.

He let them in with his key, and he saw his grandfather walking down the staircase. "Hey, Granddad."

"Hey Will. Who is this pretty young lady?"

"This is Jemma Alden. Jemma, this is my grandfather, Joshua Rutherford."

"Hello, sir. It's nice to meet you."

"Same here. How are you?"

"I'm doing well."

"Good. Hope you're hungry. We have a nice dinner cooking for your visit."

She instantly liked Joshua and smiled at him. The couple followed the older man into the sitting room where Robert was reading the paper.

"What's up, bro? Hey, Jemma."

"Hi, Robert."

"Where is Grams?" Mona walked into the room at that moment, her eyes accessing Jemma. Her complexion wasn't too dark, and she had to admit she was a pretty one, but that didn't matter. Will made the introductions, and she held out her hand.

"Hello, Mrs. Rutherford. It's nice to meet you." Mona looked at her hand before shaking it with the barest touch of her hand.

"Hello, Will, darling."

She moved past Jemma to hug her oldest grandson; the action not going unnoticed to Joshua.

"Well, let's sit down. I believe Mrs. Tylan has made a good dish tonight," Will's grandfather said, and they went to the formal dining room where the good china was sitting on a white lace tablecloth. Pitchers of water and lemonade were passed around as the soup was served first.

"Mmm, this smells good," Robert said, sniffing the hot liquid.

"I believe Mrs. Tylan was in an experimental mood today. This is a new dish—crab meat soup."

Jemma looked down at the bowl at Mona's words and saw pieces of crab meat in the brown mix. Will reached over and took the bowl away from her, placing it by him.

"Is something wrong, Jemma?" Joshua asked between bites.

"I'm allergic to seafood, Mr. Rutherford."

"Oh, I'm sorry. We can have Mrs. Tylan make something else for you."

"No, it's fine. I'll wait for the main course," she informed him, taking a sip of her drink.

Will looked at Mona, but he couldn't read her face because her head was down. He knew he had told Mona what foods Jemma couldn't eat, but maybe it was just a coincidence since this was only the first course. He put his spoon down and decided to wait for the main course with her.

"Will, it's OK. You can eat your soup." He shook his head, and Mona looked up at them.

"So, Jenna, how did you meet Will?" The older woman asked, not looking at her.

"My name is *Jemma*, and we met at the diner on campus. I'm a waitress there." Her eyes got big and sliced between the two of them.

"You're a waitress?" Mona asked in a high-pitched voice, and Robert looked at her with surprise. Jemma felt her face get hot with embarrassment at the way Mona said the word... like it was the worst possible thing in life.

"I only work part-time."

"Yeah, it's cool. Plenty of students have jobs on campus to have some extra money," Robert spoke up, and she smiled gently at him.

"Rutherfords don't associate with waitresses," Mona said with determination that seemed like it would end the conversation. *Who does she think she is?*

"Well, this one did associate himself with a mere waitress, and I'm glad he did," she said, nudging her head toward Will.

Joshua smiled and thought, *Oh, I like her!*

"I happen to be a nursing major, Mrs. Rutherford. Waitressing isn't my goal in life, so can we please move onto something else?" She felt Will squeeze her hand under the table, and she let out a deep breath.

Jemma had never met anyone like Mona; she just seemed so... horrid. She took a deep breath and had to remember she had been raised to respect her elders. Mrs. Tylan came in to take away the soup bowls and delivered the main dish of linguini pasta with sautéed jumbo shrimp. She looked at the food, and her heart sank. Will's grandmother was sending a message loud and clear... She didn't want Jemma around.

Will picked up the plate and walked out the dining room, hearing Robert say, "Since when did Mrs. Tylan cook seafood like this?"

Will walked into the kitchen, holding Jemma's plate in one hand.

"Is there something wrong with the food, William?" Mrs. Tylan asked, wiping her hands on the apron. She was a short, robust black woman who always had her short hair slicked back that was graying at the sides.

"Did my grandmother give you a list of food allergies for today?"

"No, she didn't. In fact, when I went to the store, she told me to get plenty of nuts and seafood. I even made a chocolate walnut cake for dessert. What's wrong?"

"Jemma is allergic to this," he said, holding up the plate.

"Oh no. She didn't eat any, did she?"

"No. Thank you, Mrs. Tylan."

Will slammed the plate down and stormed out the room, seeing red. What he was feeling was a million times worse than what had happened on Thanksgiving. What if Jemma hadn't been paying attention to the food and had eaten some of it? People with severe food allergies died all the time, and he bet his grandmother didn't think about that.

"Will, what's the matter?" Robert asked with concern seeing his face when his brother walked back into the room. Ignoring the question, he walked over to Mona who was chewing on the shrimp.

"Did you tell Mrs. Tylan to make food that Jemma is allergic to?"

Will asked her, who was still chewing her food while keeping eye contact with him.

Jemma looked back and forth between the family members, noticing that Joshua and Robert hadn't said anything while waiting for her to answer. Mona took her time chewing and dabbing at her mouth with the linen napkin before she sat back in her chair.

"You did give me a list regarding your friend, but you never once said not to prepare said foods," Mona countered, and it took everything Will had to not tighten the string of pearls around her neck.

"Excuse me." Jemma quietly excused herself before she got up and left the room.

Mona didn't pay any mind to the three guys who were looking at her. She saw how Will and Jemma were eyeing each other, and she made it a point to put an end to it immediately. She didn't think she'd overstepped her boundaries once Will saw that she was doing this for his benefit.

"Mona, that is foolish. Obviously, you were told so Mrs. Tylan wouldn't make those foods. What if Jemma had accidentally eaten something? She would've gotten sick," Joshua said to his wife in sheer disgust.

Robert looked at his brother and saw a range of emotions cross his face. He didn't know what was wrong with his grandmother. She was so damned focused on keeping the Rutherford name in high prestige she was ruining her relationship with her grandchildren. After counting to eighty-seven, Will felt calm enough to talk to his grandmother.

"I don't know what your problem is, but this is the last time I'm going to tell you. I do not give a damn about marrying into a good family or the girl you pick out for me. You think just because you married into this family, you can manipulate people into doing what you want. Jemma and I like each other, and until you accept her as being part of my life, I won't be back."

"William! You're not going to talk to me in that tone and dictate what—"

"And you're not going to disrespect my girlfriend either!"

He left the room followed by Robert. Joshua looked at Mona, not believing she could be this way. How had she ended up being this type of person?

"Why are you looking at me like that, Joshua? One of us has to care about preserving the family." He rolled his eyes at that.

"I care more about our grandson's health and happiness more. You forget your place, Mona. Our marriage was a convenience that *you* benefited from. The only joy you brought me was my son, who was fortunate enough to find his soul mate."

Mona was quiet at Joshua's words. He'd never spoken to her like this before, and she realized that her heart was beating fast.

"What are you getting at, Josh?"

"I'm filing for divorce," he announced, then he walked out the room. Mona sat there stunned at what he'd just said, not knowing her actions would lead up to this.

～

"GOD! Will's grandmother sounds like a real bitch," Sonya said. She was sitting next to Jemma as she was eating a bowl of cereal.

After Jemma left the dining room, she'd gathered her coat and left the house. She refused to stay one more second with a woman who clearly didn't want her there. She knew Will would be mad when he found out she had left, but she needed to get away. If she had known Will's grandmother would've acted like that, she never would have agreed to meet her.

"Are you OK?" Sonya asked, looking down at her neon colored watch.

"Yeah. I don't want to hold you from your date."

"It's OK. He can wait." The phone rang, and Sonya answered it.

"Hello?"

"Hey, Sonya, it's Will."

"Oh hey, Will. What's up?" She looked at Jemma, who shook her head. "Is Jemma there?"

"No. I thought she was with you."

"She was. When she gets in, can you have her call me, please?"

"Sure thing." She disconnected the call, and after talking to Jemma for a few minutes, she left for her date.

Jemma put her bowl in the sink and went to her room. She didn't call Will that night. She just wanted to be by herself with her thoughts. She had never met anyone like Will's grandmother and didn't think people still existed with that old-fashioned way of thinking. She took an aspirin, hoping it would make her headache go away as she lay down.

∼

LATER THAT NIGHT, Mona was sitting at her vanity table in the master bedroom, rubbing moisturizer on her hands, thinking about what had happened earlier. She didn't feel bad, but she knew Will had been serious about what he had said. She'd give him a few days to calm down, and then she'd call him to smooth things over. Her table was a dated one with the oval-shaped mirror where she could adjust the angle. It had a bronze mirror tray that held all her perfumes with the squeeze pumps and lotions. She opened her jewelry box and looked at all the expensive pieces she had in it. She knew if things got hard, she could get a large amount of money for the pieces, but she would never do that. She was in a position where she would never starve again and never go without coal or wood to stay warm in the colder months and be destitute. Her grandparents and parents had been beyond poor while she was growing up. It was five people living in a shack in the deprived town of Evans Cove, Mississippi.

Everyone in the home had to work to bring in an income, and Mona remembered picking through the junkyard for cans that could be cashed in. Her saving grace had been the fact that she was smart, and she had a teacher who saw her intelligence and talked to her parent's about nurturing it. Mrs. Oberlin had told her parents about an all-girls school in Washington, D.C. that she felt would benefit Mona in the long run as far as helping her get into college. So, for the next few years, her family had sacrificed and worked their fingers raw to save enough money to relocate and pay for tuition. Mrs. Oberlin continued to challenge Mona in the classroom until she and her parents had finally saved enough money to move. Once they had traveled, her parents had been lucky to find employment working for the same family. Her dad ended up being the head chauffeur, and her mom became the housekeeper. Going to the all-girls school is where Mona was drilled the importance of education, and the fact she had a leg up on other black girls in her position had planted a seed that slowly grew.

From that, to the hand-me-downs that were given to her by the family her parents worked for, and the fact that her parents were making decent wages, when she saw other black girls in town and how some of them couldn't even read or looked homely, Mona knew she was going to get far in life and was glad she didn't walk around looking like those girls. Because her parents lacked the intelligence their daughter had, they were more than happy to make sure they worked hard so that she could go to college.

By the time she enrolled at Howard, the school had already had a substantial female population, and Mona had never seen anything more beautiful in her whole life. She always thought it was her fair skin and intellect that caused the male students to flock her way. Mona remembered seeing the jealous looks from some women in her class, and it made her feel good because she *knew* she was better than them. Then, she met Joshua Rutherford, and everything changed.

They started dating, even though there was no spark between them. They were attracted to each other, enjoyed the other's company, but that was the extent of it. Rumor had it that Joshua was in love with a girl who worked in the hospitality department, and after his father found out, the girl mysteriously left the university. Mona recalled the look on his face when they got married a month later; it was an expression of discontent. She jumped into her role as a social butterfly immediately and didn't graduate college because she had gotten married, and it took all of her time being the privileged, powerful wife of Joshua Rutherford. When he took over the company after his father passed, and she discovered she was pregnant with their son, Mona knew she was on easy street. She dedicated her life to being the perfect mother and complacent wife.

Joshua walked into the room and stood there, looking at Mona. He had to admit she had been a beauty back in the day, but all that displeasure and misery made her look older than she really was. He loved Mona but wasn't in love with her. He never had been. The one woman he loved, Trudy King, had disappeared from his life, and he'd settled on Mona. Joshua used to think what would've happened if he and Trudy had run away like they'd planned… what their life would be like. Since it wouldn't change anything, and decades had passed, he focused on the present things like expanding Rutherford Tech Elements and being a good grandfather. Joshua cleared his throat, and Mona turned on her stool to look at him.

"Are you moving back into the master bedroom?"

"No. We need to talk about what you did earlier," Joshua announced, walking further into the room to sit on the plum colored settee in front of the bed.

"I don't want to talk about it, Josh."

"Why? 'Cause you'd have to admit that you were wrong?"

"If you say so." Joshua shook his head and took a deep breath. He had on a gray two-piece pajama set, and Mona was wearing a white silk nightgown with a matching robe.

"I was serious about the divorce, Mona. I called my lawyer earlier this evening to get the paperwork started."

Mona's heart began to beat faster at his words. She thought he was just speaking out of anger earlier, but apparently not.

"What do you want me to say?"

"You don't have to say anything. You'll be financially taken care of, but I can't do this anymore Mona. I can't keep finding ways to evade you and avoid coming home most days; I'm too damn old for that."

Joshua didn't give Mona time to respond to that because he got up and left the room. She turned back to her reflection in the mirror at a loss for words.

CHAPTER 5

A week had passed, and Jemma had been successful in avoiding Will. She made sure she'd arrived at class early and left a few minutes after the professor. She switched her days at Chit Chat's with another waitress and hadn't taken Will's calls. Ever since the disastrous dinner, it didn't seem like she could face him. She didn't want to because she knew he'd be upset at the way she left and because she was self-conscious by how she was treated. She thought they could use the time apart, but she really did miss him. It was the Friday after Valentine's Day when Jemma was taking a shower, and Sonya was getting ready for her class and study group. Will was at the door when she opened it, scaring her.

"Jesus! You scared me, Will!" she exclaimed, placing a hand over her racing heart.

"I'm sorry. Is Jemma here?"

She looked at him and felt kind of sorry for him. He was growing a beard, and his eyes looked sad. Sonya exhaled and came to a decision… only because Jemma was walking around with the same gloomy expression.

"She's here, but I don't know if I should let you in."

"I just want to make sure she's OK. She's been avoiding me."

"Yeah, with good reason. Your grandmother was horrible to her."

"I know. That's why I need to make sure she's OK." Sonya sighed and opened the door wider so he could enter.

"She's taking a shower. Can you lock the door after me?"

He did as she asked and quietly made his way to her room. The desk lamp was on, and the TV was showing a Pepsi commercial. He leaned against the desk and waited for her to come out the bathroom.

Jemma finished washing the soap from her arms, let out a sigh and decided to call Will once she was done. After turning the water off and toweling dry, she lotioned her body and walked out with a towel wrapped around her. Jemma stopped in her tracks when she saw Will in her room. They didn't say anything as they continued to gaze at one another. The modest part of her was saying to go put some clothes on, but his intense stare with that frown kept her in place.

"Hi. How have you been?"

"You've been avoiding me," he responded instead, and she cleared her throat.

"Yeah, I needed some time to myself after last week."

"So, why couldn't you pick up the phone and tell me that?" She bit her bottom lip and looked down. Will inwardly gasped at the action.

"I'm sorry, Will." She apologized softly.

"Look, Jemma, I know that my grandmother was nasty to you, and I want to apologize for how she behaved. Until she realizes that you're going to be in my life, I won't be bothered with her."

"Will, I don't—"

"It's not up for discussion about her." She let out a deep breath and nodded, knowing he was standing firm on the matter.

"I understand."

"Are you OK, Jemma?" She nodded again and stared into his green eyes, still seeing the fierceness in them.

"I was actually going to call you once I finished my shower."

"What were you going to say?"

"I was going to tell you that I miss you." She answered softly and honestly. Will stood up to his full height and walked over to her. He cupped her cheeks with his hands and ran his thumb over her bottom lip, Jemma closing her eyes at the message."

"I missed you too, Jemma," he muttered to her. She placed her hands on his arms and looked up at him.

"Please, don't do that to me again. It broke my heart when I couldn't hear your voice."

He lowered his head and touched his lips to hers. She eagerly accepted his kiss as their tongues and mouths slowly enveloped each other. She was aware of the towel over her body, but she didn't let that stop the great kissing that was going on. Will sauntered Jemma to her bed and lay down on top of her. She helped take off his t-shirt, his smooth, rippling chest was so sexy and appealing to her. Jemma moaned as Will deepened the kiss, causing her nipples to harden and push against the soft towel. Her skin had been cool after getting out the shower, but it now burned in the most pleasurable way. The hair at his navel was soft and felt good against her fingers.

"Mmm... baby, we have to stop," Will whispered.

"Just a few more minutes," she responded between kisses as he pulled apart the ends of the beige towel.

He bent down to nip and suckled at her neck, his mouth paying adequate attention to the tender spot below her ear, knowing that area was sensitive. He made his way down and closed his lips around her right, chocolate, delectable nipple. She wiggled in desire as Will's warm tongue and sweet mouth did new, wonderful, and welcomed things to her. He took his time at the generous mounds by squeezing her breasts gently and tending to both. She cradled his head in her hands, her bare legs rubbing against his jean-clad ones as she watched him at her breasts. Jemma's body had become feverish with passion and taut with unreleased yearning. She felt a throbbing need between her legs that was begging to be consumed by Will as she grasped for his belt.

"Baby, no. We have to stop," Will repeated, reaching for her hands.

She was breathing hard and looked up at him. Licking her swollen lips, she came to a decision... one she knew she wouldn't regret.

"I don't want to stop, Will," she told him softly, watching his eyes so he knew she was serious. He sat up with a visible hard-on and looked at her with wide eyes.

"Jemma, do you know what you're saying? Are you sure?" he asked with a rocky, yet strong voice.

"Yes, Will, I'm sure." He gazed into her amber eyes, and her dimples appeared like two pools of honey that he longed to taste when she smiled at him.

"Are you absolutely sure?" he asked again, and she let out an apprehensive chuckle.

"Yes."

He grabbed the back her head to pull her to him where he kissed her gently. "We'll take it slow, OK?"

"OK," she said in a calm voice.

She watched him get up to take his shoes and socks off, covering herself again with the cold, damp towel as Will turned the TV off. He also clicked off the desk lamp, pulled his wallet out, and placed some condoms on the table next to the bed.

"You always carry those in your wallet?" she asked in a saucy tone.

There was enough light coming in from outside that they could see each other in the darkness.

"Ever since Thanksgiving, yes," he replied, undoing his belt.

"That was three months ago."

"Oh, I know. Trust me."

"Wait! Let me."

Jemma stopped him as he started to unbutton his jeans. He watched as she slowly undid the button and zipper. He was at maximum overdrive between his erection and being horny. He had to remind himself that she was a virgin and he had to make it good for her. He jerked a little when she reached into his clothes to push the pants down his firm, muscled thighs. Jemma sat back and got a big eyeful of his enlarged manhood that was jutting out from a patch of dark hair at the base. She cocked her head to the side and bit her bottom lip again.

"Damn, don't do that, babe. What's the matter?" he asked her.

"You're too big. I don't think it'll work."

Will chuckled softly and took her hands. "It'll work. We'll be a perfect fit."

"I don't see how," she mumbled, once again glancing at his thick, firm dick. They stood together naked as Will wanted her to get a feel for his body, and Jemma eagerly explored his fantastic male form. Hardness rubbed against suppleness. He didn't say anything as her fingers caressed him and moved across each wonderful inch of his impassioned skin. He had to admit that it did feel good to have her hands all over him, and he knew it would be even better to have her pressed against him in bed.

"You have such a nice butt," she said, pinching his behind.

"Thank you. I'm asking again, are you 100% sure about this?" Jemma leaned up and pressed a kiss to the pulsing vein in his neck, under his chin. "Yes, Will. Make love to me."

He wrapped his arms around her waist as their lips connected again. She became dizzy with delight as Will increased the kiss as they made their way back to the bed. The virgin in her was excited this was finally happening since she didn't know how much longer she could hold out against him. Jemma wasn't sure she wanted to anymore and hoped that this was everything she'd dreamed of. His hands traveled down her body to cup her womanly area and found her wet. Jemma closed her eyes and moaned as Will's thick fingers stroked her, easing them back and forth...up and down across her throbbing nub. He leaned down to tend to her breasts again by sucking the hardened nipples and teasing them. After getting his fill, he moved lower to kiss her stomach and lick her rib cage. Jemma figured out what he intended to do, and she pushed at his shoulders when he got eye level to the peach fuzz between her legs.

"Will, no. Don't," she protested, her heart beating swiftly.

"It's OK, Jemma," he reassured her, and she nervously licked her lips, her chest rising and falling at a rapid pace as he continued to nibble and peck his way around her pulsating middle.

She gasped when he placed gentle kisses on her inner thighs, glad the room was dark so he couldn't see the deep flush covering her face. Her legs had a mind of their own and automatically opened for him.

Will took that as a sign to proceed, and he hooked her legs and applied the first lick between them. No coherent thoughts or words came to Jemma as he suckled and slurped her distended clit. Will loved her faint whines as he feasted on her. Her strained sounds egged him on, and since she didn't know what to do with her hands, she covered her eyes, and her hips began to move in circles on their own accord. Will could have sworn that he'd never tasted anything so sweet and mouthwatering. Her scent kept calling out to him as time became an unimportant factor while he pleasured her with his mouth.

Sheer enjoyment was shared by both parties, and she was surprised that they kept at it. She thought it would be a few licks and kisses, and he'd be done after that. But being down there for a long time, she realized she'd never experienced anything this delightful before. Lick. Swirl. Gyrate. Flicker. His wide, flat tongue was doing all that and more, and she hadn't known that she said, "Don't stop," in a raspy voice. Jemma had nothing to compare this to, but if she was grading him, Will would've gotten an A plus. Her very first climax left her body shaking and quivering at each tongue-lashing, and she felt like crying and laughing at the same time, her body feeling like pins and needles. Will sat up with a soft grin, his cock pounding a thousand times painful, and she stared up at him with her tawny eyes shining with longing.

"Are you OK?" he asked with one hand on her leg and the other arm braced beside her head on the pillow.

"Yes. That was... It felt..." He smiled in understanding when she couldn't finish her sentences, and she reddened again.

"There's more where that came from."

He leaned forward to kiss her some more leaving her hands free to roam over his body as they slid down his chest and further down to wrap her fingers around his long hardness. There was a softness to it, yet it was rigid at the same time. It felt like velvet wrapped around a steel rod and Will cursed as he reached for a condom. He swiftly ripped open the foil wrapper with his teeth and sheathed himself. He heard her chuckle, and he looked at her, settling himself between her bent legs and the sheet was resting on his lower back.

"What's so funny?"

"You're in a hurry."

"That's cause I'm about to burst if I don't feel you soon," he said, wrapping his fingers at the hilt so he could guide himself.

Her laughter was replaced by a gasp when he entered her inch by magnificent inch.

"Oh, God." She moaned, her appearance showing a mask of pain. Will cupped her face as his thumb ran down her cheek, a small part of him glad that she wasn't crying. He stopped when he was halfway in to let her get used to the feel of him.

"The pain will go away in a second, baby." She cupped his cheek with her hand a few minutes later.

"It's fine now."

"OK. I'm almost in."

"You have some more to go!"

"I'm sorry, but you deserve every inch of this, honey," he told her and kissed her forehead, easing completely inside until he was at the base.

"You're trying to split me in half," she murmured softly as her nails were digging into the flesh of his arms.

"I promise I won't," he replied as he began to move back and forth slowly. Jemma groaned at the movement and closed her eyes, turning her head to the side.

"No, look at me, sweetheart."

She did as he said, noticing the pain had indeed faded away, and satisfying waves took its place. It was uncomfortable at first, but after she got used to his stroking and length, it began to feel amazing. In fact, it seemed like he filled an emptiness inside her that slowly began to build into an awesome sensation she never felt before. Something intense and tingling washed over her, responding to Will's profound thrusts. They kissed one another in feverish consumption to match his increased tempo, his big hands gliding over her heaving breasts. Will broke the kiss and tossed his head back as he continued moving strong and powerful inside her gushy warmth until they both had spine busting orgasms.

WILL WOKE up the next morning with Jemma snuggled against him. He was pressed against the wall, and her head was resting under his right forearm. He saw that it was gloomy outside with dark clouds from the window and grabbed the comforter that made its way to their feet. He glanced at the clock on the desk and saw that it was 7:12 a.m. He wrapped his free arm around her stomach and settled back on the pillows as he thought about the previous night. If Jemma were a drug, he'd be an addict. Her taste was beyond scrumptious, and after the initial pain, she turned into a little hellcat in bed with all the scratching and biting she had done.

He counted six orgasms, which was remarkable for a novice. This was the first time he deflowered a virgin, and he was honored that she had chosen him to share this special moment with. He remembered how tight and wet she had been, and he wanted to be greedy and keep at it all night, but he knew she would be sore and she had to rest. Just thinking about how good she felt around him caused Will to get hard again, and the blanket had slowly bucked upwards.

"Good morning. You look deep in thought." Will looked down and smiled, not knowing she had woken up.

"Good morning. I'm just recollecting memories from last night." She blushed at his words and cleared her throat, not saying anything for a few seconds.

"What about it?" she asked in a small voice.

"It was—Hey, look at me." She lifted her head and made sure she kept eye contact with him. "It was wonderful, babe." She smiled at his words, pursing her lips.

"Yes, I know. I didn't...I didn't know it could be like that. You made it very extraordinary, Will. Thank you."

"Thank you for letting me be your first."

She pulled her arm from under the blanket to cover his chest, and she saw his erection tenting the bedspread. He ran his hand down her tousled hair when she licked her lips and looked up at him again.

"Is this a typical day reaction?" she asked with a sly grin.

"Usually, yes, but you're the reason this morning, babe."

"Hmm, is that right? Well, let me help you do something about it since I'm the reason you're sporting morning wood," she said as her hand slid down his stomach to disappear under the sheets. Will let out a deep, chesty rumble when her soft fingers enfolded around him.

"You're not too sore, Jemma?" he asked in a low voice as he moved over to climb on top of her. Jemma shook her head, wrapping her free arm around his neck while the other hand was slowing stroking him under the sheet.

∼

"Hey, Will, you know what I was thinking? We should spend the summer at the beach house." He looked up at Robert's words and nodded.

It was the first week of May, and the school year was slowly coming to a close. They were in the living room studying for finals with the windows open to let in the spring breeze. The radio was on, and the station was playing "Bernadette" by The Four Tops. Will still hadn't been by to see his grandmother since the disastrous dinner, even though he had spoken to his grandfather a few times. After the initial lovemaking, Jemma and Will had only gotten together three times after that, and he was feeling antsy.

"The whole summer?"

"Sure, why not? We can invite Brandon, have some fun on the beach, go swimming, take in the bikini girls, and bring out the grill. Junior year will be hard for us; might as well relax before it begins." Will sat back in his chair, just as Brandon walked in from the kitchen with a ham sandwich.

"I heard bikini girls. What happened?" Robert chuckled and shook his head.

"Little brother was just saying we should spend the summer at the beach house in North Carolina," Will filled him in, and Brandon responded with excitement.

"Hell yeah, count me in! I'll spend a few weeks in Baltimore with the family, but after that, I'm on board."

"What about Jemma?"

"I'll ask her. She'll be over in a few minutes."

"So, how are things going between you and her?" Brandon asked Will, and he grinned, thinking how far their relationship had progressed since their first meeting at Chit Chat's.

"Things are great."

There was a knock on the door, and he got up to answer it. Jemma walked in with her book bag slung over her shoulder, grinning when she saw Will.

"Hey, guys," she greeted the others once she walked into the apartment.

"Hi Jemma," they repeated in unison. She stood on her tip toes to give Will a kiss on his cheek. She had on a blue jean floral skirt with a white top.

"Hey Jemma, talk to your girl for me," Brandon said, turning around to face her with one arm hanging over the back of the chair.

"About what? You're not her favorite person."

"I know. Just tell her to call me sometime."

"I'm not sure if she has your number."

"She has it," Brandon said with conviction.

Jemma looked up and saw Will nudge her with a 'come here' motion with his head, and she followed him to his room where he closed the door.

"You trying to get with Sonya, man?" Robert asked Brandon, who had just finished sharpening his pencil.

"No... Yes... I don't know. Hell, man, she's not like the other girls I mess with."

"You mean she doesn't swoon at your feet, and it ticks you off."

"Well... if you want to use those exact words, sure." Robert laughed and headed toward the kitchen.

In Will's room, the stereo was up with enough volume to block out the groans coming from Jemma. She was on his bed with her skirt around her waist, and Will's face was buried between her legs after pushing her underwear to the side. He wasted no time rushing her to his room and getting to what he wanted. He was craving the nectarous taste she possessed, and he wanted it on his tongue right now. Her shirt was open, and he was caressing her lace clad breast. She bit her bottom lip as he did that swirly thing with his tongue that she absolutely loved. Her left leg was resting on his shoulder, and for some crazy reason, it drove Will nuts when she tightened her thighs around his head. Her skin was hot with desire and lust as a fierce climax flooded over her in blissful waves. Will stood up and multitasked by undoing his jeans and flipping Jemma over on her knees. She gasped because this was a new position for her and because he had given her a hard slap on her behind; the anticipation of them joining again causing her heart to beat erratic.

When he saw what she had on under her clothes, Will was clearly pleased with the matching purple bra and thong set, and he gently cupped her ass. He put on a condom and let out a breath of satisfaction when he slid inside her. He could've sworn he felt her insides latch onto his flesh and gradually draw him inside her sweetness. Jemma's fist was gripped tightly in the sheets, a soft cry escaping her lips as he began to move inside her. *Oh, God... this feels so good!* she thought. She was becoming a wanton. She wanted to stay like this as long as she could get it. To have Will completely filling her, making it feel beyond fantastic. His hands were cradling her waist as he was pounding into her with steady thrusts. He liked seeing her ass cheeks jiggle with his movements and stepped closer to the bed so he could go all the way inside. Her breasts were moving against the bed, and her nipples were pushing against her bra, causing them to swell with each rub.

"Oh, shit!" he roared when her hips began to move back and forth to join his shoves, and she flexed her inner muscles around him.

"Damn, baby!" She looked at him over her shoulder and gave him a grin that reached down to his center. *She knows what she's doing*, he thought, and that gave him all the motivation to keep providing the surefire thrusts, needing to feel her erupt all around him.

JEMMA HAD a stunned look on her face, shocked by Will's words.

"You want me to come to your beach house?" The euphoria from their lovemaking had worn off, and they were in his bed, lying face to face.

Will's jeans were on, but unbuttoned, and she had fixed her clothes, so they were right again. She still wasn't comfortable being naked around him, even though he'd repeatedly told her she had a beautiful body.

"I would like you to come, yes. Rob and I inherited it from our parents. My dad purchased the land and built the house for my mother because she loved the beach. It has two floors with five bedrooms with private bathrooms, a wraparound porch, and a huge sunken living room. The beach is a few feet away from the back door, and it has a firepit facing the water."

Jemma smiled at the description, knowing he was probably thinking about the good times there with his parents.

"It sounds wonderful, Will, but I can't spend the whole summer there."

"I know, honey. I know you'd want to spend some time with your aunt. What about coming a few days before the Fourth of July and stay for a week? You can ask Sonya too; she might like it."

She agreed with that and thought about it. *Hell, why not?* She'd never spent the summer on the beach, and the water with the sun rays would be so relaxing. She also had never traveled to that state before and thought it would be fun to go.

"OK, Will, that'll be great. Thanks for the invite," she whispered.

"Thank you for accepting," he returned, easing his hand down to her butt. The image of her in a cute swimsuit got him all hot and bothered, and she saw the evidence making itself known in his jeans.

"You ready to go again?" she asked, shimmying her skirt up over her hips.

"Now, you know you don't have to ask me that," he replied, leaning over her to capture her lips in an unhurried kiss.

OVER THE COURSE of the next few weeks, finals had been completed and the sophomore year had ended. The students were looking forward to the summer vacation, and the teachers were ready for the three-month break. Jemma and Sonya planned to fly to North Carolina the week before the holiday; the latter super excited about the trip. The couple had bickered because Will wanted to pay for her plane ticket and she wouldn't let him. After coming to a compromise, she was OK to let him pay for her ticket back home. On the last day of school. Sonya left for Atlanta and Jemma went home after spending the day with Will. Paris thought it was a good idea for her beloved niece to go to North Carolina and had taken her shopping trip to get some new clothes for the vacation.

CHAPTER 6

Jemma was bubbling with enthusiasm as she looked out the window and saw the plane make its way to the airport. She and Sonya had planned to meet at baggage claim and wear pink, so they could easily spot each other. She had on a strapless pink and white sundress with white sandals on. She was so anxious to see Will, her best friend, and spend some much-needed relaxation on the beach. Grabbing her travel tote, she moved with the line to exit the plane with the departing flyers. The airport was a decent size, and people moved about quickly as she walked toward baggage claim. Grabbing her bags, she looked around for the color apparel until she saw Sonya coming out the women's room wearing a pale rose babydoll top with a mini skirt. They ran toward each other, smiling and hugging once they met.

"Look at you!"

"I'm so happy to see you."

"You know I have to borrow that dress, right?"

"You think you have packed enough?" Jemma asked, looking at her friend's three suitcases.

"Now you know how I travel; one can never have too many clothes. How's your aunt?"

"She's OK. She's in Vegas with Stan having a good time. How are your parents doing?"

"They're good. Daddy is doing great as a congressman, and my mom thinks he might run for Senator."

"Really? That's great."

"Yes, it is. She was helping organize a park cleanup that he was spearheading when I left."

"That's cool. I like your parents, and your dad is such a decent, honest man," Jemma told Sonya as they made their way toward the main entrance, thinking about the few times they had come up for parent's weekend or dropped Sonya off at school.

"I know, and they're still hot for each other. Girl, I caught them going at it in the library! They didn't see me, but I was in shock for like seventeen hours." Jemma laughed at that and Sonya soon joined in. "That's funny. Now, you know you want to be like that with your husband at that age."

"Oh, please! I need to graduate first. I didn't go to school to get an MRS degree. Now, to change the subject… Where is your hottie of a boyfriend? I'm starving!"

"I don't know. He said he'd meet us here." She said, glancing at the huge clock behind the ticket counter that showed 6:27 p.m.

"Jemma!" She turned her head and saw Will approaching from a few feet away.

She smiled and waved at him, her dimples showing with a radiant smile. He had on cargo shorts and a red short sleeved shirt. She was so ecstatic to see him! They hadn't laid eyes on each other since he left campus in May and although they had spoken on the phone several times, it wasn't the same as seeing him in person. Will finally reached them and gave her a quick peck on the lips. Jemma was a little stunned at the chaste kiss he had given her; she thought it would be more amorous given the weeks they spent apart.

"Hey, beautiful. Hi, Sonya. Brandon is waiting by the car." They followed him through the crowd to head outside through the front doors with Will carrying one of their bags each in his hand.

Brandon rushed to help once he saw the group approaching, and the guys loaded the luggage into a black CJ-7 Jeep with the doors and roof off.

"Is this yours, Will?" Sonya asked.

"No. We rented it for the summer," he answered as he navigated onto the street away from the airport traffic.

Jemma was sitting up front next to Will and Sonya was in the back with Brandon. She glanced in the side mirror and saw him lower his head to whisper something in Sonya's ear, and she rolled her eyes with a tiny grin. Will grabbed Jemma's hand and rubbed the back of it against his cheek as he drove the vehicle with his left hand.

"Hey," she said with a grin.

"Hi. I missed you, Jemma."

"Me too, Will."

"You're going to love Mavis Pointe. In addition to the beach, there's shopping, a boardwalk with rides and attractions, and downtown tours."

"I'm sure I'm going to love it."

"Hey, Will, can we stop for some food? I'm so hungry," Sonya said the last part in a high-pitched voice.

"We put burgers on the grill for dinner for you ladies," Brandon replied, looking at her.

Will glanced over at Jemma and saw her looking at the sites. He couldn't wait to get her alone to kiss her good and proper. He liked that dress on her and how great her legs looked in it. Twenty minutes later, he pulled up in front of a big house that was painted white and baby blue with a porch swing. Leaving the bags in the car, they got out, and Will decided to give them a quick tour. They were shown the big living room with a big Ivory sectional couch that went well with the patterned carpet and a big screen cable TV. The dining room was behind it with a huge open kitchen with two bathrooms on the first floor. He showed them their rooms next to each other with their individual baths. Sonya flopped down on the big queen bed in her designated room, and Will took Jemma's hand and pulled her to his room which was at the end of the hall.

He closed the door as his lips greedily covered hers. She cupped the back of his neck and wrapped one arm around his waist. Her face was cupped in his big hands as he continued the deep kiss. It was time-consuming with both sets of lips and tongues wanting to get reacquainted with one other. Jemma felt her nipples get hard and began to ache in addition to feeling Will's erection pressing against her stomach. Will moved his hands up under her dress to grope her ass. He was glad he was able to feel her skin because of the thong she was wearing.

"Damn, I missed this," he said against her lips, yanking the dress down from her breasts.

He took one of the buds into his mouth and wrapped his warm mouth over it, his tongue moving up and down the nipple. Moving to the other one, he paid it just as much attention, and she squirmed against his body gasping loudly. She reached down toward the zipper of his shorts and starting to rub him through the material. After a quick tug here and a shimmy there, Will had lifted Jemma against the door and entered her. The union was intense and raw as he moved back and forward inward. The sounds of flesh pounding in the flesh were accompanied by Jemma's moans and Will's grunts. She wrapped her arms around his neck and held on for dear life as she felt him grind in and out her buzzing core. His hands were on her thighs to keep them where they were. Will let out a harsh curse against her bosom when he felt her milk him. Jemma had an explosive release, and he came a few minutes afterward. Her head landed in the crook of his neck with her hands resting on his shoulders. Both were breathing hard and fast.

"Are you OK?" he asked with a gruff, dry voice, and she nodded.

"Did I hurt you?" she replied with a shake of her head.

"Why aren't you saying anything?"

"I'm trying to catch my breath," she wheezed out, and he chuckled.

"I wanted to kiss you like that at the airport, but I didn't want to cause a scene." He told her, and she smiled at that. Will was still buried inside her, and he leaned forward to kiss her again. She licked the shape of his bottom lip before covering them.

"Can I sleep in here tonight?" she asked against his lips in a murmur.

"If you want to," he replied as he started a slow grind of his hips back and forth. Jemma broke the kiss. The feminine and soft mewling moan she emitted in his ear caused a rippling effect of trembles to go down Will's back.

∽

JEMMA HAD JUST WARMED up her second hamburger and walked back to the dining room where she watched everyone else play spades. It was going on eleven pm, and a cool, refreshing breeze was making its way through the house via the open screen doors and windows. There was a boombox on the counter, and a local radio station had just finished playing Queen.

"Hey, Sonya, you need to play your hand. We could've won that last game if you played your cards right," Brandon said to her, and she scowled at him.

"Well, if you stop cutting my cards, we could win a game." She returned, and he let out an irritated breath.

"Well, if you—"

"Hey, you two are partners. You might want to work together," Robert interjected so they could stop arguing.

"Naw, let them keep bickering. Two more, and we win the game," Will said to his brother who grinned.

Jemma threw her paper plate away after watching the next round and went to go stand at the door. She unquestionably loved the breeze and the sounds of the ocean. *I could stand here all night.* She watched a man walk along the sand with a dog who kept fetching the ball that was being thrown. Jemma had left a message at her aunt's hotel to let her know she had arrived safely after her reunion with Will. Letting out a big yawn, Jemma headed upstairs to take a shower. A few books later, the brothers had won the game, and Brandon and Sonya were still trading barbs at the table.

"I think those two should have at it," Robert said, drinking from his bottled water, and Will laughed. They were sitting on the porch steps enjoying the wind.

"You ever think about mom and dad when we're here?" Robert asked Will, who was leaning back on his elbows.

"All the time, bro. What's up with that girl you were talking to on the beach yesterday?"

"Nothing, just casual talking. Why aren't you upstairs with Jemma?"

"Giving her some time to shower and get settled. We still going to the store tomorrow?"

"Yes. We should ask the girls if they want anything."

"OK. I'm off to bed. Goodnight, Rob."

"G'night. Don't you and Jemma break the bed," Robert replied with a smile.

"Oh shut up, dipshit." He walked back in the house and up to his room. The light was off, and he saw Jemma asleep in the bed. Will went to the bathroom to shower and climbed into the bed after drying off with a pair of basketball shorts, wrapping his left arm around Jemma and pulling her close to his body.

~

JEMMA WOKE up in Will's arms, and she smiled softly as she turned toward him, gently running her fingers over his sleeping face. His bedroom was a decent size with two windows on the north and east walls. The bed was placed so when he laid down, he was looking at the beach. A black round rug with stripes was in the middle of the floor, and there was a recliner in one corner that sat across a tall, five-tiered dresser. She had slept well last night due to the plane ride, good loving and ocean gusts. Will sighed in his sleep and she chuckled lightly when he made a face. After kissing his cheek, she quietly got out the bed and headed downstairs. She saw the front door open, and Sonya was sitting on the porch swing with her robe on.

"Good morning," Jemma said, going out to sit next to her best friend.

"Hey. Good morning."

"Are you OK?"

"Yeah, I'm fine. Why?"

"Because it's eight in the morning and you're sitting on the porch by yourself."

"I'm just enjoying this beautiful view." Jemma nodded, seeing the people from the city clean and comb the beach.

"It is a pretty sight. How did the card game go last night?"

"We lost because I had the worst partner ever," Sonya answered, folding her arms over her stomach. Jemma laughed, shaking her head.

"Anyways, we hitting the beach today, right?"

"Of course. I have this super cute swimsuit I bought," Jemma responded.

"It better not be too cute. Your boyfriend will likely have a fit."

"He'll be fine."

"Speaking of which… I see how you two stare at each other. Y'all are clearly crazy for one another."

Jemma smiled and blushed, watching the waves crash against the shore. A part of her was glad her affections for Will were transparent to other people, and Sonya's sentiment was correct; she was gaga for her man. Actually, it went way beyond that…

"I love him, Sonya," she confessed, and the other girl's mouth dropped open, causing Jemma to giggle at her facial expression.

"You love him? That is so cool!" she shrieked and hugged Jemma. "Have you told Will? What did he say? When did it happen?"

"Well, I haven't said anything to him yet, and as far as when, it was after that incident with his grandmother. He was such a gentleman and caring and patient. He was so concerned with my feelings and wanted to make sure I was OK." Jemma recalled that point in time, remembering how concerned and worried he was about her.

"Aww, that's so nice. I bet he's a pistol in the sack too." Jemma nudged Sonya, who grinned.

"I'm not telling you that!" Jemma was all for telling her best friend certain things, but the special, intimate moments with Will...she'd keep those to herself.

"You don't have to; you have creaky furniture," Sonya replied, laughing at the surprise on Jemma's face.

"So, why are you up so early?" Sonya asked after having her laughing spell.

"I was going to cook breakfast, but now I'm thinking about getting a new bed," Jemma mentioned, her tone sarcastic at the last part.

"Are you making your famous pancakes?" Sonya asked in a giddy tone. She *loved* Jemma's pancakes.

"I can. Let's go see what they have in the kitchen."

The two women went into the kitchen, and Jemma found the ingredients to make pancakes, eggs, and they had turkey bacon. Sonya made the coffee, and Jemma looked at her.

"You know, you're gonna have to learn how to cook something besides chili and coffee." She shrugged as she set the table.

"I'll learn how to cook after I graduate."

"Well, just in case, you better marry a guy who can throw down in the kitchen," Jemma told Sonya, who made a face.

"You think we should go wake up the guys?" Sonya asked as she placed a platter of scrambled eggs in the middle of the glass table.

"I would think all these enticing smells would wake them up," she replied.

Just then, the men walked downstairs. The two brothers were slipping on t-shirts.

"What smells so good?" Robert asked, sitting down at the table.

"Just breakfast I put together real quick," Jemma answered, joining everyone at the table.

"This looks good, babe. You didn't have to do all this," Will said, looking at her.

"It's OK. I don't mind," she replied, smiling at him.

The five of them kept of lively conversation as they ate. Brandon volunteered to clean up everything, and Jemma noticed that Sonya was looking at his muscular back as he did the dishes. An hour and a half later, the guys left to go to the store and the girls headed for the beach. Sonya had on a white and blue swimsuit with ruffles across the bodice, and Jemma was wearing a peach polka dot two-piece suit. They laid towels on the beach chairs to sit on them after applying sunscreen.

"This is so great," Sonya said, and Jemma agreed with a grin.

She wore a pair of sunglasses and was enjoying the sun. Sonya noticed guys looking their way and took note of the people out and about. Old and young folk were already out appreciating the day by swimming in the ocean with inflatable toys and playing games in the sand and surfing. A few yards away were a bunch of college-aged kids playing beach volleyball with the three nets that were up, and grills had been set up in the designated area; the scent of grilling meat in the air.

"You want to go look around with me?" Sonya asked Jemma, who had turned around on her stomach.

"No, I'm good right here."

She wanted a nice, even tan and she was liking the idea of just laying around, soaking up the sun rays. She didn't hear Sonya leave and assumed she went off to explore the area. A few minutes later, Sonya came running back over to Jemma, and she bounced down on the foot of the chair.

"Hey! I just met two cute guys, and they're putting together a volleyball game with their sister and some of her friends. They need some more players. You wanna do it?"

Jemma sat up and looked over Sonya's shoulder and saw two guys walking toward them. They were medium height, had small Jheri curls and were cute like Sonya said, but they had nothing on Will.

"C'mon. Let me introduce you." Sonya grabbed her hand and pulled her to meet the guys halfway.

"Jemma, this is Patrick and Paul. Guys, this is my best friend, Jemma."

"Hi, it's nice to meet you," she said, shaking their hands, noticing Paul had held onto her hand longer than necessary.

"So, Jemma, are you up for playing with us? You and your girl will even our team out," Paul said, smiling at her.

"I'm not really good at it."

"Oh, come on, Jemma. It's just a friendly game," Sonya pleaded, giving the side eye to Patrick.

"Yeah. Besides, whoever my sister gets on her team will suck anyway. It'll be an easy win," Patrick said, and Sonya giggled.

"Sure. Why not?"

The two girls went to get their things as the brothers talked amongst themselves. Jemma slid into a pair of blue jean shorts, and Paul watched as she wiggled her behind into the clothing, and he inwardly smiled. *Oh yeah, she's going to be mine*, he thought. They walked down the beach to where people were standing around waiting for the game to start. Introductions were made, and a few minutes later, the game got underway.

Back at the house, the guys walked in carrying eight bags full of food. After putting the groceries away, Will found Jemma's note saying she and Sonya were on the beach, and he went to look for them after changing into some swim trunks. Will scouted the area and found them in the middle of a volleyball game, glad they had met some new folks. Will slowed his steps when he spotted a guy give Jemma a high-five and throw his arm around her shoulders. *What the hell?* Jemma turned her head, saw Will, and she ran over to him.

"Hi, honey!" she exclaimed, wrapping her arms around his waist.

"Hey. What's going on here?" he asked with his gaze on the guy who was eyeballing Jemma.

"Sonya found some new friends, and they asked us to play with them."

"Yeah, that one looks like he wants to do more than play volleyball with you," Will said, nodding toward Paul who finally looked away from them.

"Don't worry about it. Let's get in the water," Jemma suggested, leaving the game behind after excusing herself.

They stayed on the beach all day, swimming, playing, eating, and listening to music. Different people had all types of sound systems out, and a variety of tunes could be heard throughout the day. Even after the sun went down, it was still activity on the beach. Half of the parking lot at the end of the beach houses had emptied by nightfall, but people were still lounging about. A big bonfire had been built, and there were several people hanging around it that included a guy who was playing an acoustic guitar.

Will and Jemma were walking hand-in-hand as they made their way toward the fire. Jemma had on a white jumper with no shoes and Will was wearing a gray tank top and blue sports shorts. Brandon was walking around with a sulky attitude because Sonya had spent all day with Patrick. Jemma inwardly shook her head at that situation, hoping whatever it was would pan out. Will placed a small blanket down on the sand and they sat on it, with Jemma sitting between his legs. The guitarist finished a rendition of "My Girl" by The Temptations, and he bowed after getting some applauds.

"As I was saying before our musical break, this is a great place to get married and raise a family," Paul stated, directing the last part at Jemma, whom he was looking at.

"Do you not see me sitting here?" Will asked him, and Paul diverted his attention to the conversation next to him; Jemma leaned back and kissed his cheek.

Even though they had talked to the other teenagers and college-age students, Will kept his eye on Paul, who was steadily looking at Jemma. She finally pulled Will to his feet, and they started walking along the beach away from the action after sensing he was seconds away from punching the shorter dude in his face.

"This is so lovely," Jemma said in a soft voice, looking up at the dark sky that was filled with stars.

"Not as lovely as you," he said to her, wrapping his arms around her lower back.

They leaned into each other for a kiss that was sensual and good. She lightly moaned and was caressing the back of his neck with her fingers.

"Mm... You always taste so sweet," Will said with a low growl, causing her to step back and lick her lips.

"What's wrong, baby?"

She let out a deep breath to calm her racing heart since she was about to say something she'd never said to a man before. She didn't know what his reaction would be, but she knew she didn't want another minute to go by without letting him know how she felt. She told herself it was no big deal what he would say, but she knew that was a lie.

"I love you, Will," she told him, holding eye contact, gently biting her bottom lip, and hoping he wouldn't laugh in her face.

She didn't say anything as he cupped her face and brought her hard against his body where he kissed her again with all the passion and emotions he possessed. *She loves me!* Will picked her up and spun her around in slow circles on the sand.

"Say it again."

"I love you, Will Rutherford," she repeated against his lips.

He was not expecting Jemma to proclaim her love for him and didn't expect the warm feeling of joy to float over him after hearing the words. Hell, maybe a small part of him needed to hear her say it. Jemma had given him her most treasured gift and he loved spending time with her. He loved that she was hardworking, motivated, intelligent, sensual and funny. He pulled back to look at her and swiped his thumb over her succulent bottom lip.

"I love you, too, Jemma." She stared at him with wonder and happiness, grinning at his words.

"You do?"

"Yes. How could I not? You're classy, gorgeous, smart, assiduous and you're mine. You fit me, Jemma." He placed soft pecks on her neck, and she moved to give him more skin to pay attention to.

"Say it again," she mumbled, tossing his words back at him.

"I am so in love with you, Jemma," he repeated, and her eyes teared up at the spoken words.

"Perhaps we should move things inside," Will recommended when their kiss became hot and heavy that included sexual squeezes and kneading.

∼

BACK AT THE beach house in the privacy of Will's bedroom, Jemma let out a saucy smirk as she started to unbutton her jumper. Will had sat down in the recliner chair in the corner after removing his shirt.

"Honey, can I ask you a question?" she asked, kicking her clothing to the side and tugged her panties down her hips.

He nodded, his head cocked to the side as he got an eyeful of her tanned, breathtaking figure. Jemma walked over to him and kneeled between his open thighs. She leaned forward and began to place open, damp kisses across his chest, paying distinct attention to his flat nipples. Will got hard when she lapped and softly bit them. He ran his hand through her loose mane when she smooched him lower and was kissing his chest and stomach, the faint hair tickling her nose.

"What's your question, sweetie?" he prodded in an uneven voice.

"That thing that you do when your head is between my legs... can I do that to you?" Jemma asked, undoing his pants and reaching inside to grab him, causing Will to let out an inward hiss.

"I think I created a monster," he grumbled instead of answering her question, watching her pull his shorts down. A frown was set on his brow as she was using both hands to touch and fondle his impressive penis.

"You did. It's all your fault," she agreed with a cute smile, and he tweaked her chin.

"Mmm... Well, my apologies, my love."

"Don't say that. I love you, and I love when we're together in that way," she reassured, slanting over him to kiss his cheek. "Now, about my question..."

"If you want to... yes."

"And I can do it how you do with the suckling and everything?"

Will's mind went blank at her inquiry, positive that he was having the best dream of his life. She was previously a virgin and he knew she was asking out of curiosity. But the way she asked with her eyes all big and innocent; it drove him crazy. He nodded a response and felt himself grow harder at her inquiry.

"Just think of it like you're eating a chocolate popsicle," he voiced, and she deliberately moistened her lips from one side to the other with the tip of her tongue while looking down at his throbbing manliness.

"Or an extra big blow pop." Will roared with laughter at her words, and she joined him.

The lights were off in the room, and they were able to hear people still having fun on the beach from the open windows. She settled back, hunched down, eyeing his massive erection.

"You sure you want to do this, Jemma?" she acquiesced and could feel herself already getting wet between her legs accompanied by a powerful ache.

"I want to please you like you do with me, Will," she confirmed, rubbing his velvety soft tip across the tops of her breasts that were exposed by her bra.

Jemma lowered her head, and Will knew it was over at the first feel of a timid swab on his delicate tip. All the nerve endings seemed to double in size at the attentiveness, and once she found her rhythm with his coaching, it wasn't long before she became proficient at the task. When she added her hand to match her up and down activity, he clutched the sides of her head with both hands and grabbed her hair. For this to be Jemma's first time giving head, she was on point. She changed her suckling techniques from hard to soft, mixed up the speed from fast to slow and her mouth was extra watery and sloppy.

"Fuck!" Will closed his eyes and threw his head back, rumbling when she lowered her head to play with his testicles. "OK, that's enough."

He stood her up and sat her astride on him, her legs bent at the knees behind him, so her privates were nestled against his.

"Why did you stop me?" she asked as he took her bra off and his thumbs ran over the curves of her tits.

"Cause you're driving me insane with that mouth of yours, and I want to be inside you when I bust this nut." Will's words turned her on more, and he grabbed her by the back of her head and pulled her forward to his waiting lips. "Did you like what you just did, babe?" he asked as his hands were running up and down her back in a fondling motion that was causing shivers to cross her skin.

"Yes. You tasted yummy." She wrapped her arms around him and rubbed her chest along his strong one; making her nipples peak into firmness. He moved one of his hands between their bodies and felt her arousal on her outer lips.

"You're so ready for me... That's a good girl."

Jemma shuddered as he ran a thick finger over her exposed clit, and Will thought he'd never been so fucking hard in his entire life like he was now. She was moving her hips back and forth on his dick, spreading her juices over it. He was without a condom and feeling her skin-to-skin was incredible.

"I need to get some protection, Jemma," he said around the nipple that was in his mouth.

"It's OK this time. I'm on the pill," she returned, needing him to be inside her right now.

He placed his hands on her hips, easily penetrating her, and she released a soothing sigh. They both took a moment, needing to get used to the feel of them being intimate without any protective sheath; the feel of flesh embedded inside flesh. It felt different... more rigid, solid and fulfilling. Jemma started an up and down motion with the help of his hands on her waist.

"You have no idea how good this feels," she moaned in a whisper in his ear, biting the earlobe.

"Oh, I know, honey. I swear your pussy was made for me."

She smiled at that. Her skin hummed at his words. She placed her hands on his shoulders and switched to a faster pace by bouncing on him. Will tried to slow the thoughts in his head to keep himself from exploding right now. Jemma was clearly putting it on him, and he wanted to enjoy it as long as possible. Their bodies became sweaty with perspiration filled passion, and it was oh, so fabulous. A low, squeaking sound erupted from Jemma while she was having the best orgasm. Strained veins were visible in Will's neck as he pumped to a tremendous release. An extra amount was extracted when she milked his nine inches of goodness. Having sex without a condom had been the best experience, and Will felt an obsession coming on to always end up in her rubber free.

"I honestly think you tried to suck the life out of me with that last one," he rasped, and she chuckled when he wrapped his arms around her.

"I didn't. It... you not wearing a condom... it felt amazing," she confessed, and he kissed the top of her head.

"I know, babe. I feel the same way."

A few minutes later, they had gotten off the chair and moved toward the bed where they slumped down on top of the cool coverlet. Jemma was laying on her stomach with her arms under her chest, and Will was stretched out on his side facing her with his left hand resting under her tush.

"We're supposed to be enjoying our summer vacation, and here we are going to sleep before midnight like old people," Jemma said, glancing at the clock which showed 11:17 p.m.

"Who says we're sleeping?" he countered, and she smiled. "We can go back outside if you want to."

"No, I'm OK. Besides, I feel like you might punch Paul in his face, and I don't want you to get into a fight."

"As long as he stays away from you, I'm cool."

"Do they usually have fireworks for the fourth?" she asked, changing the subject.

"Yes. The city puts on a show that can be seen from the beach or boardwalk."

"That's nice. What are we doing tomorrow?"

"We can go into town. You and Sonya can look around and do some shopping."

"Sounds like a plan." He reached up to stroke her lips, and she licked the digit.

"I wonder if it's bad that I think about sex with you all the time," she commented out loud, and he laughed.

"Are you turning into a nympho?" She shrugged one shoulder and sat up on her arms.

"No, it's just that since we started having it, I want to do it all the time now." Jemma lay closer to him, and he snuggled with her.

"It's not uncommon given it's something new for you. I don't want you to walk around sore from all the lovemaking, but I am happy to oblige in any way I can."

He let her know, and she jokingly rolled her eyes. "I bet you are." Before she took her next breath, Will was poised on top of her and had her hands pinned down next to her head.

"Is that sass I'm hearing from you?" She rubbed her legs against his rough hairy ones and arched her back so the tips of her tits brushed his chest.

"It was just a tiny bit of sass," she admitted with a satisfied, and he sneered at her. "In that case, I think I need to find a better use for your mouth."

THE NEXT MORNING, Jemma was up making breakfast for everyone again by preparing French toast, eggs, and hash browns. As she was turning the bread, she smiled thinking about how she had woken Will up hours ago. She was getting used to this oral sex thing. Maybe it was because she liked doing it, and it was such a turn-on for her. She glanced out the window in the kitchen when a loud clap of thunder shook the house. It had started raining a few hours ago, and by the looks of the dark clouds, it wasn't letting up anytime soon. As the potatoes were cooking, she quickly set the table and put out a pitcher of orange juice. Will came down and headed toward her.

"Good morning, honey."

"Morning, Will."

"You know you don't have to cook breakfast every morning, right?" He had a tone, and she stared at him with a hand on her hip.

"I know, but I don't mind. Can you build a fire?" She turned her back to him as she grabbed the spatula. After Will made a big fire in the sunken living room, he went back to the kitchen where he wrapped his arms around her stomach from behind.

"I'm sorry," he mumbled, kissing the side of her neck.

"It's fine. Just because it's our vacation doesn't mean we pig out on pizza and cereal. Honestly, it doesn't bother me, Will." He kissed her cheek and went to go wake everyone up.

They ate the tasty meal, and the guys cleaned up the dishes. The girls had showered and were in the living room talking while the guys were in the kitchen preparing the menu for the holiday feast.

"All this rain is making me gloomy," Sonya said, adding another log to the fire.

"Yeah, I know. It was supposed to be a shopping day."

"Hopefully, we can go tomorrow. You think they would want to go rent some movies?" Sonya asked, pulling her knees up on the couch.

"That sounds fun since we're stuck in the house." The guys walked into the room to sit down, and Robert was holding a pad and pen in his hand.

"So, what's on the menu for the holiday?"

"Burgers, chicken, corn on the cob, potato salad and spaghetti," Robert read off the list to the ladies, and a loud clap of thunder and lightning followed.

"And who's going to be the one grilling?" Jemma asked as Will left the room.

"We're going to take turns," Brandon responded. After a few minutes, Will came back in, and Robert looked at him.

"What's up, bro?"

"Nothing. I just gathered supplies in case we lose power."

"Do you think that will happen?" Sonya asked with concern, looking at Jemma.

"I don't, but we're prepared just in case."

"We should go rent some movies since we can't go anywhere." Brandon curled his lips and rolled his eyes at Sonya's words.

"And who is supposed to drive out in this mess?" he asked, and she sighed at him.

"I wasn't asking you, pretty boy." Robert chuckled and shook his head.

"I can see this is about to turn into another argument. If you want to go, Sonya, I'll take you."

"Thank you, Robert." She mean-mugged Brandon and headed upstairs to change.

"I'll go with you. She's likely to rent all chick flicks," Brandon said as he went to go look for an umbrella.

"This is going to be a fun drive with those two," Robert muttered, and Will chuckled.

He waited until Rob left the room, and Will looked at Jemma, who was sitting on the sofa chair with a throw pillow on her lap.

"You want to go with them?"

"No, I'm good," she answered.

"Are we OK, Jemma?" he asked, and she nodded at him. After showering, Will had put on green sweatpants and a white t-shirt.

"And don't think we're getting nothing but macho guy movies neither," Sonya said as she put on a jacket with a hood. Apparently, their disagreement was still going on, and it didn't look like it was letting up anytime soon.

"And girlie, sappy movies are something we want to look at all night?" Brandon replied, following her out the door.

Robert let out an exaggerated breath and walked out the house with the keys in his hand. Even though it was going on one in the afternoon, it was very dark, and it looked like it was night time.

"Those two are a trip," Will mentioned, looking at his girlfriend.

He was sitting on the floor with his back to the couch, and his legs were crossed at the ankle. She grinned and placed her head in her hand.

"You sure we're OK?"

"Yes, honey. Why do you keep asking me?"

" 'Cause you're usually chattier than this."

She rolled her eyes and threw the pillow at him before standing up. She had on a baby blue tank top and a matching cotton skirt that stopped above her knees. She went to grab the remote control off of the low TV stand, looking at the few pictures that were on the bookcase. She bent down to look at the rest of the photos, and Will tilted his head, openly eyeing her round butt. Seeing her delicate, exposed skin got him rigid, and his erection poked against his sweatpants.

"Shit," he whispered, licking his lips while reaching inside his pants.

Even the barest glimpse of Jemma got him all hot and bothered. He could safely say that he'd never had this type of reaction with a woman before and was glad it was with the one he was in love with. Jemma turned around and gawked when she saw Will fondling himself out in the open. She watched as he was moving his right hand up and down his hard length, and she instantly started pulsating between her legs, especially when she saw the tip was shiny with pre-cum. She was hypnotized when he continued to jerk off and wanted to replace his hands with hers.

"What are you doing?" she asked in a strained voice, and he shook his head. "Nothing, just sitting here." He noticed her eyes were glued to his penis and hadn't strayed from what he was doing.

"What got you in that condition?"

"You bent over and I saw some skin."

"Oh, geez!" She rolled her eyes and laughed, walking toward him.

Everything went by in a flash as she took over his hand with her mouth and after a few minutes, Will showed her a new position by having her do the reverse cowgirl on him. It was awesome because they were in a common area in the house, and it was an unfamiliar way for them to get it on that they both ended up enjoying on several levels.

~

THE NEXT DAY was a perfectly sunny day that didn't have a single dark cloud in the sky. A nice, cool breeze was blowing over the area as Jemma and Sonya were in town doing some shopping. Jemma had on white shorts and a pink colored sleeveless top while Sonya was wearing an orange summer dress. The downtown district looked like Small Town USA with an antiquated feel that the girls loved. It had cobblestone streets, the old-fashioned hanging street black lamps, several different colored benches that were placed in certain spots around the area. The storefronts were painted white and American flags decorated most of them while red, white and blue bunting decorated the fountain that stood in the middle of town square. Locals greeted them as the women went from store to store and did some window shopping.

"This is cute!" Jemma exclaimed, holding up a pale red thin strapped dress with a white ribbon over the middle.

"It is. You should buy it," Sonya added, glancing at the article over her shoulder; Jemma looked at the price tag and decided to purchase it.

They were in a quaint store called Mavis Pointe Boutique, and it was a nice shop with reasonable prices. After the transaction was made, they walked out and continued to stroll around. Both girls had shopping bags in their hands, and Jemma hoped Aunt Paris and Stan liked the gifts she bought them.

"This has been a great day. I love this little town," Sonya declared as they sat down at an ice cream shop. They had a few minutes before they were picked up. The guys chose to forego the three-hour outing. The girls were sharing a hot fudge sundae complete with nuts and whipped cream.

"I agree. What's going on with you and Brandon?" Jemma asked, and her friend shrugged.

"I'm doing what he suggested. We're just friends, and we hang out with other people. He doesn't like when I do it, but it's OK for him to walk around chilling with other females."

"Are you two together?"

"No. It's just a lot of heavy flirting between us."

"You two should just do it and get it out of your system," Jemma suggested, and Sonya shrugged again.

"That's not going to happen. He's so damn arrogant."

"So, it's just going to be all this back and forth with you two?"

"Yep. We're going to be friendly for the rest of the trip." Jemma sighed and scooped up a dab of vanilla ice cream.

"Well, as long as you're OK and no one's feelings will get hurt." Sonya popped the cherry into her mouth before changing the subject.

"So, how are things with you and Will?"

"It's going good. We love each other; we're extra hot for each other."

"Yeah, I know," Sonya mumbled.

"Don't tell me you can hear us!"

"No, but it doesn't take a genius to figure out what you guys are doing when you both sneak away." Jemma chuckled, her face becoming hot. It was only a handful of people in the air-conditioned eatery, and there was soft elevator music playing in the background.

"Hey, I understand. You two are young, in love, and horny. I say get as much of each other as you can, especially when school starts back. It's going to be super busy for our third year." Jemma agreed, and they continued talking until Robert picked them up at the souvenir shop where he dropped them off hours ago.

∽

Brandon found a parking spot a few feet away from the pier, and everyone got out after agreeing to meet at the car when the boardwalk closed. Will and Jemma chose to walk together to the end of the pier which was empty from people. Small waves crashed against the wood pillars and sandy shores. Her heeled sandals echoed on the wooden walkway, and the sun was starting to set which made the receding rays stunning against the sky.

"You look so gorgeous in your new dress," Will told her, enclosing her in his arms with her back against the waist-high plank.

The music of Duran Duran was coming from the boardwalk, and the colorful lights from several games and rides were reflecting off the water. It hadn't gotten crowded yet, but in about an hour, the place would be crawling with people looking to have a good time.

"Thank you, Will. You're looking extra manly, honey," she said, sniffing his neck. She got a whiff of his zesty cologne. He had on acid washed jeans and a gray t-shirt, his muscles in his arms and back pressing nicely against the fabric. He smiled at her words, bending down to press a kiss to her cheek and she ran her hands down his back to rest them on his waistband.

"You drive me crazy, Jemma," he pronounced softly, gently nibbling at her ear.

"You do the same with me." She gasped when he slightly lifted and raised her left leg.

"Will... we can't... not here." She wrapped one arm around his neck as his hand caressed the inside of her thigh, causing amazing ripples to cascade over her skin.

"I know, baby. I'm just getting a quick fix until later." He wrapped his free arm around her waist as he shimmed the top of her dress down with his teeth.

"I would ask what's going on later, but I already know." She moaned with pleasure when he inserted two fingers inside her.

"I love how you're always so juicy and ready for me." She brushed her lips with her tongue and shifted her legs open for him. Her forehead rested against his.

"Since you seem to know what's going on tonight, know that you're going to ride me long and slow. But before that, I'm going to show you another way to fuck."

"Is that what we're calling it now?"

"Right now, yes," he responded, running a finger over her stiff bud.

"Two ways?" she repeated in a little voice, peeking over his shoulder to make sure they were still alone, her lower body jerking with each hand thrust.

"Yes. You're young; you can take it." Jemma laughed at him, which turned into a moan when he increased his hand movement. Will watched her face as she had a shattering orgasm, his prick throbbing something fierce.

"Hmm... that's what I like," he said, looking at the wetness slide down her thighs.

Her head rested on his shoulder as her body repetitively jerked and spasmed. He pulled his fingers out and mouthed the digits.

"You're insane," she mumbled against his body, and he smiled.

Will leaned forward to kiss her at a leisurely pace and pulled back after a few minutes. Jemma could spend all day and night kissing Will and not get tired of it. He was so good at it, and she enjoyed it with him.

"Say what I want to hear."

"I love you, Will."

"That's my girl. Jemma, I know we have a lot going on with school and have a rough road ahead of us, but after graduation and we get into our respective careers, you're going to be my wife." She gasped at his words and watched his eyes, knowing he was serious.

"Will... I..."

"I'm not proposing now. Just letting you know how things will be."

She smiled at his assured words. A small part of her jumped for joy at his words. She knew Will would make a great husband and life would be so wonderful with him. Will watched as various emotions passed over her face while she sorted out his words, and he was glad she hadn't run for the hills.

"You're so confident about that."

"Damn right. You love me. I love you, and I'm not about to let any other guy have you. Call me traditional, call it taking charge, but I'm claiming you as my wife."

Something inside her exploded with jubilation and happiness at what he said. She loved the idea of them having a future together. They'd only been dating for ten months, but they had so much chemistry, passion and good communication that Jemma felt like they were soul mates.

"You care to comment on what I just said?" he asked when she had been silent.

"I like your plan. The fact that you want us to wait until we're done with school is great. I don't want any other guy, Will. You're so good to me. You make me laugh, and you're respectful. You've shown me how two people can express their love with their bodies and hearts. Thank you for that."

He glowed at her words, giving her a quick kiss on the lips. "C'mon, let's go have some fun."

After spending hours enjoying themselves on the boardwalk, Will won Jemma a stuffed animal, they had taken pictures in one of those old time photo booths, they shared a root beer float, and the group went back to the beach house around midnight. As soon as they got in, Jemma went in to take a shower and went to bed. Brandon, Robert, and Will were in the kitchen getting things ready for the cookout. An hour later, foil covered meat was placed in the fridge just as Will placed the dry ingredients on the counter.

"These ribs and burgers are going to be great with my famous homemade BBQ sauce tomorrow," Brandon mentioned, washing his hands.

"I bet. I'm going to hit the sack."

"Me too." Will got to his room and saw Jemma asleep on her stomach. He went to go wash the day's dirt away, his body still burning from their earlier encounter. Will climbed into the bed naked and leaned over her to nibble at her neck, knowing she liked it when he kissed her there. Jemma shifted in her sleep as his hand slid under her t-shirt. His warm hand eager to stroke her soft skin.

"Wake up, baby," his deep voice crooned in her ear, and she lifted her shoulders when his breath tickled her warm skin. Jemma rolled over on top of him, and both sighed with gratification when he slid inside her, and she started a slow back and forth rocking.

The next day produced a comfortable eighty-degree temperature for the Fourth of July. The beach was packed to capacity with extra lifeguards and police patrolling the area. People started to arrive at nine am to start the grilling and to make sure their seats were secured for the grand fireworks show that would take place once the sun went down. The college group was in good spirits that day, and the three guys took turns manning the grill. Jemma decided to help by making the potato salad. Since Sonya wasn't that great of a cook, she appointed herself to make sure the drinks were kept cold and the condiments were replenished and darn it... she did an excellent job of the task. The fireworks show was an amazing event as people ooh'd and aah'd over the colorful, bright explosions in the sky. The couple sat on the porch as they watched the fireworks, and they both knew this was the best Fourth of July they ever had. Will wrapped his arm around Jemma and kissed her head. His girl smiled and rested her head on his shoulder. The five people were glad to have the chance to relax and have some fun before junior year began, which they knew would consist of hard, demanding work, but they were looking forward to it.

CHAPTER 7

Walking into the library, Jemma found an empty table to study for her human anatomy class. The teacher was a tough-as-nails instructor and had given them a test on the first day worth twenty percent of the grade. Per the teacher, it was "to weed out those who couldn't cut it!" It was three weeks into the semester, and she was clearly feeling the workload from all her classes. Her medical terminology class was easy, but her anatomy and human development classes were kicking her butt. She liked the challenge and knew she had to put in extra study time for them. Things had been so busy on her end, and she could just imagine Will's homework with all his courses. Between his criminal justice, government disposition, and sanction sessions with the general education classes, they hadn't been able to spend any time together. They did talk on the phone every night, but amid papers that had to be written, group presentations, and study groups, no couple time could be squeezed in for them.

She knew he had a mock trial coming up in a few weeks, and she made sure she put it on her calendar to be there for him. Jemma took her books out her bookbag and let out a deep breath at the long study session ahead of her. Two hours later, across the campus in the law library, Will let out a strained pant and ran his hand over his eyes after the words began to swim before them. It was a five-story building that had every medium available needed for legal assistance and aid. In addition to standard tables, cushioned benches were placed through the building for those who needed to have additional space to study. It was one of the oldest buildings on campus, and it showed with the ancient interior design and speckled pillars that ran the height of the place. He glanced around and saw that it was packed for a Friday night. The majority of the student body was excited because over the summer, the campus computers had been upgraded to include the first version of Windows from Microsoft. It was making typing papers and storing information better for the pupils. Will's criminal justice class was the hardest one in his opinion, but he had to admit that it gave him a rush learning from the textbook and the teacher.

His professor, John Sachs, Esquire, was a top-notch lawyer, and he announced to the class that they would get their mock trial cases, in addition to informing them who be the prosecutor or the defense the next time class met, and Will was excited about it. Looking at his watch, he saw that it was 9:30 p.m. and decided he was done for the night. He'd been at it for three hours, and his brain couldn't take any more. Will began to pack up his bookbag when Kiara Spooner walked up to him. She was as tall as him and had the girth like an Amazon woman. She was in his criminal justice class, and she was a pushy little thing. She'd shown attention in Will since class started, and he'd made it clear that he was not interested in her. She had bombarded herself into his study group and even suggested they have a private study session at his apartment.

"Leaving so soon, Will?" she asked, standing next to him, wearing an outfit that screamed "look at me" and was too inappropriate for the weather.

"Yeah, I'm all studied out."

"We should go get some coffee to unwind."

"You can't unwind on caffeine, Alicia."

"I meant decaf, silly."

"No, thank you." He finished his task and turned toward the double doors to leave, and she injected herself in front of him.

"Oh, be nice, Will. It's Friday night, and it's still early. We can compare notes," she prompted, thrusting her chest toward him. He had to stop himself from rolling his eyes.

"No, I'm good. Now, excuse me," he said forcefully as he stepped around her and walked out the building.

He didn't get these women who couldn't take a hint when a man wasn't interested. *Like seriously, have some pride about yourself.* Erasing the recent encounter from his mind, Will wondered if Jemma was at home. She and Sonya had left North Carolina a week after the holiday, and with the semester three weeks in, it had been damn near six weeks since they'd seen each other, and he missed her. Will hurried to where his car was parked, and he made a quick stop at home before heading toward her place.

~

JEMMA LET out a deep breath as she turned off the kitchen faucet. She had just cleaned up the few dishes in the sink after eating a hotdog and French fries. After getting some hard-core studying done, she went home and fixed dinner after taking a hot shower. Sonya had left dressed for a date and told Jemma not to wait up. Since they were now upperclassmen, their living accommodations had been upgraded to an off-campus apartment. It was bigger than the dorm, and it gave them plenty of space where they weren't crowded all the time. They lived on the first floor, and their neighbors were nice. The apartment had a kitchenette area and attached bathrooms to their bedchambers, so they didn't have to share anymore. It had a decent size living room that had enough space for a small couch, two built-in desks, and a metal TV stand with the radio setting on a table by the window.

Last semester, the two of them had discussed living off campus and had decided as long as everything was split fifty/fifty, they'd go for it. Jemma was walking toward her room when she heard a loud knock on the door. She gasped and grinned when she saw Will through the peephole. Quickly opening the door, she didn't have time to greet him before he rushed in and kissed her. Cupping her face, Will tongued the hell out of her, using his foot to shut the door. Jemma kissed him back with just as much urgency as he was dishing out. She broke the kiss and led him toward the bedroom as she licked her lips.

"Is Sonya here?"

"No."

"Good."

He lifted her up and pressed her against the wall, and she fumbled with his belt. Their lips attacked each other in a hasty kiss. Seconds later, he had roughly entered her, causing her legs to lock around his lean waist. The hallway filled with sounds of Jemma's throaty moans and Will's baritone grunts. Turns out, this position was their favorite one because Will was able to control the pace, and Jemma liked being dominated whenever he did. The union was raw and primitive as he pumped inside her slickness with deep, controlling lunges. After they both had their climax, they sagged against each other as their uneven and panting breathing matched the rapid pulse in their veins.

"Are you staying the night?" Jemma asked against the skin of his neck.

"Yes."

"Awesome." He smirked and walked them into her bedroom with his jeans around his ankles.

∼

JOSHUA GOT of out his silver BMW and walked toward his grandson's apartment. Being on campus brought back a lot of memories… both good and bad. Of course, some modifications had been done on campus to keep up with the current times, but Joshua could still see his younger self walking the grounds with his friends, being young, and not having a care in the world. After being buzzed in, he ascended the stairs, undoing the zipper to the light jacket he was wearing, and wondered how the boys would take the news he was about to deliver.

"Granddad, this is a surprise," Robert mentioned as he opened the door and gave the man a hug.

"I hope I'm not bothering you guys," Joshua said, following Robert into the living room. Will was sitting on the couch, going over his note cards for class.

"You're always welcomed here," Will replied, standing up to give the tall man a bear hug.

"You want something to drink?"

"Some water will be good." Robert headed to the kitchen, and Will looked at his grandfather. He noticed the man didn't look tired or unhappy anymore. In fact, Joshua looked healthy and cheery.

"So, what's going on?" Joshua's youngest grandson asked after giving him a glass of water.

"There are a few things I want to discuss with you two, but first, how is school going?" Joshua had on tan trousers with a navy cotton sweater.

"It's going OK. I have a mock trial coming up next week."

"That's exciting. Are you ready?"

"Yes, I believe so."

"OK. Let me know the outcome of it."

"Yes, sir."

"What about you, Robert?"

"Everything is fine, sir."

"Still no major?"

Robert inhaled deeply and glanced at his older brother before answering Joshua. "Actually, I'm thinking about Psychology. It might be useful for the Marines."

Will watched Joshua, noting his right eye twitched at Robert's announcement.

"The Marines?"

"Yes, sir. I'm going to enlist after college."

"And then do what?"

"See where the military takes me, sir." The older man was quiet as he let the news settle, taking a big gulp of water. It wasn't the ideal or suggested career choice for his grandson, but he wasn't in a position to forbid it.

"Anything to say, Granddad?" Robert asked, darting his eyes to Will, who gave him an encouraging nod.

"You're an adult, Robbie, and I support whatever decision you make. That was the last thing I expected you to say, but just be careful, son."

He nodded and looked briefly away. He was glad he had the older man's favor.

"How have you been? Is everything OK, granddad?" Will asked, and he nodded.

"Yes. That's why I came over. I hate to talk about such a delicate subject with you two, but you're grown men now. You both know that my marriage to Mona was out of convenience and I thought my affection for her would grow over time, but it never did. We're not happy together, and I haven't been in a long time. The only joy I got out the marriage was your father... I swear, I miss that boy every day."

They saw their grandfather shrink into melancholy as he thought about his only child, and it was unsettling because they had never seen him like this before.

"I don't want to spend what's left of my life miserable and going with the flow with Mona. So, I have filed for divorce," he announced and knew he had shocked them by their facial expressions.

Divorce was a rarity after forty years of marriage. Usually, people would want to work it out or try any avenue to fix their marriage problems, but Will and Robert had a feeling that Joshua hadn't wanted to go that route after dealing with Mona and her ways all these years.

"Wow. Really?" Joshua nodded, taking another sip of water.

"You're supposed to be able to look back at your married life and think of all the good times and memories with your spouse. To reflect on how you've grown and built as a unit. Mona has always been obsessed about money and setting out to prove she's better than everyone else because she's a Rutherford. I can only think of bad recollections with her. I'm more than willing to give her a nice settlement, but I can't be with her anymore," Joshua explained, and his grandsons understood.

Will and Robert were past the age where they hoped their grandparents would work things out and stay together. They knew how Mona could be and didn't blame Joshua for his actions.

"What will you do now?" Robert asked softly.

"Continue to be CEO of the company and improve with the times. I moved out of the house and into a condo. I'd love if you two could come over someday; I could put some steaks on the grill."

"Wait, you moved out?" Will repeated, and Joshua nodded.

"Mona can have the house since it's paid for."

"It's just weird to think of you as a single man after being married all these years," Robert told him, and Joshua cleared his throat as he thought about that.

Joshua was actually seeing a woman who was two years younger than him. It was funny because they'd met in a hardware store as they were both looking for a toolset. They'd been on a few dates, and he had the best time with her. Just thinking about Patti and their dinner plans tonight brought a smile to his face.

"I'll be OK with that," he said, replying to Robert's last words.

Will was quiet but not surprised by the news. He had seen how his grandparents were growing up, and he was glad that Joshua had decided to make sure he didn't spend any more time being despondent. Joshua Rutherford was a good man and deserved nothing but pleasant things in his life.

"There is one more thing. You know our annual fundraiser dinner is coming up that the company has every year at the country club. Would you guys mind going in my absence?"

"You don't want to go?"

"Honestly, no. I've been to enough of those things, and I don't want to give Mona the wrong impression by showing up." His grandsons agreed to go, and Joshua smiled.

"Thank you. It's a black-tie affair, and it's a month from now. You two can take dates if you want." They nodded, and the three of them spent the next hour talking and laughing at anecdotes until Joshua left for his date with Patti.

"What do you think about what he said?" Robert asked Will as they watched Joshua pull off in his car from the living room window.

"It's crazy, but I can't say I blame him." The youngest Rutherford nodded as he continued to look out the window.

"Yeah, I agree with you." Will slapped his brother on the back and went back to his note cards.

~

"Tell me, Mr. Farrow, do you think that people take the time to have their homes properly inspected before they purchase them?" Harold Hendricks, the "prosecuting" lawyer, asked the witness, and Will stood up.

"Objection, Your Honor! The witness can't speculate how everyone goes through the homeownership process."

"Overruled. Proceed, Mr. Hendricks."

Jemma wanted to jump up and applaud every time Will did something right during the mock trial. She had never been to the law department of the university and was surprised by what she'd seen. There was an actual courtroom staged for the trials; complete with a real judge and working multimedia center in case it had to be used. She knew the law students could appreciate this simulation because it could help with their confidence and let them know how things could go in an actual courtroom once they passed the bar exam. When Will had interrogated the "witness," he had asked all the right questions, and Jemma knew his professor was making notes from the way his left hand was rapidly moving across the yellow legal pad.

The mock case was one of a man who claimed that an electrician who had worked on his new house caused the fire that broke out after the worker had been working on the wires hours before the inferno. There was even a man sitting next to Will, who was wearing a suit, looking attentive and upset. Jemma was happy she could see this side of Will, and she knew he would make an excellent lawyer. After going back and forth with the witness the prosecutor called in, Will had surprised everyone by bringing in the chief fire inspector to determine the actual cause of the fire. Jemma knew Will had this in the bag, especially when the other guy was fumbling with his notes and not as professional as his counterpart. After the witness stepped down, that concluded everything, and their teacher stood up and approached the front of the courtroom with his legal pad in his hand.

"Do you have anything to add before I start, Judge Dorfman?" the older white woman shook her head as she took a sip of water.

"No, I'm sure we're thinking the same thing, counselor."

"Thank you for participating, Your Honor."

"You're welcome. I liked what I saw today from Mr. Rutherford."

Jemma let out a big smile and knew Will was bursting at that compliment. Professor Sachs looked at his pad again then looked up at Will and Harold. He was a tall Jewish man with a bald head and a thick, black trimmed mustache and always wore a Western-style tie. He was very strict with his students about his classes and what was expected of them.

"Gentlemen, you have been in my class for weeks, and you know I don't sugarcoat things. Mr. Hendricks, if I were your client, I would be asking for new representation. You were unprepared, fumbling about, and not focused. You hold someone's life in your hands as their attorney, and that's an enormous responsibility. With that being said, you damn sure better know the facts of the case and leave no stone unturned. Your grade is a F, and I want an eight-page paper explaining how, had you actually prepared, you could have won this case; due tomorrow by noon. Am I not clear on anything?"

"No, sir," Harold replied in a somber tone.

"Good. Mr. Rutherford, I can tell you're serious about this profession and took the time to prepare and research. It was a good idea to bring in an outside source to determine the cause of the fire. Also, your interrogations were concise and effective. Your grade is an A. Keep going like this, Mr. Rutherford, and you'll have a winning streak with your cases."

"Thank you, Professor Sachs."

The teacher stepped up to the railing and addressed the rest of his class. "Make no mistake, people; this is the make it or break it point. If you are not prepared, do not come in here and waste time. You all have your scenarios, and I expect nothing but the best. We will discuss this case in our next class. Enjoy the rest of your day."

Jemma stood up with everyone else and watched as some classmates went over to congratulate and question Will. She smiled secretly as he laughed and talked to those individuals. Minutes later, the crowd thinned out, and Will walked toward Jemma. He had on a dark blue suit with a white button down and a smoke blue silk tie.

"Congratulations, Will. I am so proud of you. You should've heard —" Her words were cut off when he grabbed her hand and led her out the room. She was wearing a plaid jumper with a white short sleeved shirt under it.

"Will, what's wrong? Are you OK?" she asked once they were in his car.

"Yes, I'm fine, honey. I'm ecstatic."

"Do you want to talk about what just happened?"

"Later, Jemma. I need something more important." Will was feeling like he was on top of the world and wanted to celebrate with his girl.

He parked his car, and they were walking into his apartment seconds later. His roommates were out, which is why he pulled her to him and kissed her deeply. He cupped her cheeks, and she eagerly kissed him back as her heart raced from the embrace. Jemma could feel the insistence in his kiss and knew he was transferring his jubilant feelings into it. He had won his mock trial and gotten great accolades from his teacher. He had walked them into the living room, and his hands had made their way under her jumper to squeeze and caress her tush. His touch left her skin scorching and her nipples pebbled against the satin material of her bra. She pushed his jacket off his broad shoulders and shuddered when his hand moved around to her front and made its way between her legs.

Digging his way inside her thong, Will found Jemma wet and feverishly stroked her wet flesh. Normally, they would take their time, but there was an anxiousness in the air, and she didn't mind it at all.

Will stepped back and turned her around, so she was bent over the couch. Jemma felt him push her clothes up and soon Will had plunged inside her. Her legs were spread open, and he was between them, pushing in and out her at a fast pace. Jemma was glad the apartment was empty because she was unable to hold in the sounds that were erupting from her that was brutal and loud, signaling how extreme their copulation was. Jemma came extra hard when he took hold of her arms and used the grip to gyrate deeper. Her boyfriend emitted a strong and forceful ejaculation.

~

The second Will got to the fundraiser he wanted to leave. He didn't want to rub elbows with the snotty and uppity folks, but they had promised their grandfather. People were coming up to him and his brother talking about the event and the company. Apparently, the trimester numbers were at an all-time high, and the investors were more than pleased with the news. Jemma couldn't make the event because she had a big anatomy exam scheduled that day, and it was the first time she was going to use a medical mannequin. Will knew how important that was to her and he didn't mind that she had to miss the party. Felicia was there with her parents and had yet to make a move on Will, but that didn't stop her from following him with her eyes all night. The gathering was a swanky one that was held at the country club ballroom that easily fit the three hundred guests.

There was a live band, and a mediocre dinner was served that consisted of baked chicken, rice, salad, and roasted vegetables. Will and Robert decided to split up and cover the room; the brothers figuring the faster they made their rounds, the sooner they could leave. Felicia watched as a waiter took Will's drink order and leisurely followed him to the bar where she made the pretense of studying the non-alcoholic list. She let out a sly grin when the waiter went to bus a nearby table, the distraction affording her the opportunity to pour a white substance into his club soda and gave it a quick swivel. Keeping eyes on her personal cocktail as the waiter delivered the drink, she made her move toward Will after seeing him take a few sips.

"Hi, Will," she purred, sitting at the empty table with him as some of the guests were dancing, talking at other tables or mingling in general. He nodded his head toward her and drank more club soda.

"I JUST WANTED to tell you that this is a very lovely fundraiser and good job on a successful night."

"Thanks."

"So, would you care to join me in a dance?"

"I'm not going to do that. You know I'm dating Jemma," he said with an eye roll, glancing around the room for his brother.

"Does that mean that you can't enjoy a short waltz with me?"

"Yes, it does, Felicia. Excuse me."

She looked at him over her shoulder as he headed toward the exit. She made sure to stay close to him when the drug kicked in... which she saw happening when he staggered at the double doors. Felicia motioned to the freelance photographer, who had been hired by Mona, to follow her. Will was leaning against the wall, holding his head. He felt fuzzy and hot at the same time. He was sweating, and his clothes were constricting on his skin. She walked over to him and saw that his pupils were dilated, and his eyes were drooping.

"Are you OK, Will?" Felicia asked as she pressed her body up against him.

The ecstasy she had given him had Will sporting a hard erection, and his skin was so hot, he felt like a furnace. He rubbed his hands down her frame, grasping her flat behind. She smiled triumphantly as Will kissed her, hearing the camera shutter take multiple pictures.

"Mmm... Jemma." She stepped back at his words, frowning at what he'd just said.

"Will, what the hell are you doing?" Robert asked, rushing toward them.

Someone had told him that Will had left the room and Robert was going to find him so they could leave. Robert had had enough of shaking hands and meeting tons of people whom he wasn't going to remember tomorrow. He couldn't believe what he was seeing and knew something wasn't right.

"He's OK. I'm taking care of him," Felicia told his brother, wrapping her arms around his neck.

Robert pushed Felicia away, not noticing the skinny man who slipped away with a camera around his neck. He looked at Will and became concerned when he saw how glazed his eyes were looking.

"Will, what's wrong?" Robert asked, lightly slapping his cheeks. He mumbled something, and Robert looked at Felicia.

"What did you do to him?" he asked, grabbing her arm.

"Stop it! You're hurting me!" She wrestled free from him and ran away from the brothers. Robert turned back toward Will just as his legs failed him, and he slid down to the floor.

∼

"Is he going to be OK?" Robert asked as a doctor was writing something in Will's chart.

"Yes, but we're going to keep him overnight as a precaution. The main thing I was worried about was getting his heart rate back to normal. It was a good thing you brought him in when you did." Robert looked at his brother, who had an IV in his arm and a nasal cannula in his nose that was dispensing oxygen.

His anger increased as he thought about what could've happened from the drug Felicia slipped him. He didn't know why she had done it, but as soon as Will as up and about, they were going to track that bitch down and get some answers. He had called their grandparents and informed them of what happened. But told them not to come down to the hospital since it was after midnight and Will's condition had stabilized.

"Would it be OK if I stayed with him, Dr. Baker?" the middle-aged doctor smiled and patted Robert on the back.

"Sure. I'll have a nurse bring you a pillow and a blanket."

"Thank you." Robert went to go sit in a chair by the bed as he let out a deep breath, the bowtie hanging undone down his shirt. He was glad that Will was going to be OK. He didn't want to think about the outcome if it had ended up a lot worse. Robert had lost his parents, and he honestly didn't think he could survive if he'd lost his brother too.

~

"WHAT THE HELL were you thinking? Drugging my grandson wasn't part of our plan, stupid child!" Mona paced the living room as she glared at Felicia who was frowning at the old woman.

Mona was nursing a glass of Cognac, the ice cubes clinking against the glass as she was striding across the floor. Luckily everyone in the house was asleep so their conversation couldn't be overheard.

"How else was I supposed to get the pictures, Mona?"

"We agreed to get Will drunk. Not for you to put him in the hospital!"

"You know he doesn't drink. You should've come up with a better plan! I knew this was not going to work the second you approached me about it. All this to break Will and his girlfriend up."

Felicia's white cocktail dress was wrinkled, and the makeup had long since worn off. Felicia had arrived at Mona's house as soon as she had hung up with Robert after giving her an update on Will's condition. Felicia had to admit that the old lady's acting skills were superior; as if she was really concerned about Will's health. Felicia had no idea how Will would react to the drug. When she had taken it, it had done wonders for her libido and she never had so many orgasms with whoever she'd slept with that night. She'd used the same dealer from the city, and he didn't raise an eyebrow when Felicia had asked for his most potent brand.

"I didn't hear you complaining when you saw that check for twenty-five grand." Felicia shrugged and looked at her fingernails.

She technically didn't need the money and would've done the deed for free. But when Mona automatically offered her the substantial sum, she jumped at the chance to take the money. Who in their right mind would refuse a check for that amount? Mona saw how nonchalant Felicia was and she stalked over to her where she grabbed her forearm, her nails digging into Felicia's skin.

"Listen to me, if something happens to Will, by the time you get out of jail, you'll be in menopause," Mona threatened with icy, hostile words, and Felicia felt a smidgen of her wrath. She pushed away from her and looked at Mona with wide eyes.

"This is your crazy plan. I'm not taking the blame for this!"

"You changed the strategy when you decided to bring drugs into the equation. Now, keep your mouth shut and let me move on to part B." Mona left the room, and Felicia wondered why she got involved with Will's demented grandmother in the first place.

∼

THE NEXT MORNING, while Will was still recuperating, Mona got out her town car and headed toward Jemma's place. Due to the Rutherford's being major contributors, it didn't take much prodding on Mona's end to find out where Jemma lived. It was quiet for a Sunday morning, and Mona had to admit she was impressed with the new changes on the campus as far as the landscaping and additional buildings that had been erected. However, she was here on a mission: to eradicate Jemma from Will's life. Mona regretted the way things went south, but once Jemma was out Will's life, he'd thank Mona and let her find the perfect woman who would balance him out. Finding the correct door, Mona knocked and waited a few seconds before it was opened.

"Mrs. Rutherford! Good morning. What are you doing here?" Jemma asked, wrapping a robe around her.

"Good morning. May I come in?"

"Yes, of course." Jemma allowed her entrance, knowing she was assessing the clean apartment with her eyes.

"Would you like some coffee?"

"No, this is not a social visit. Here." Mona handed Jemma an envelope, and there was a frown on her face as she looked at the elder woman. Sonya came out her bedroom and leaned against the wall, Mona returning Sonya's greeting in a bland manner. Jemma opened the parchment; gasping when she saw a check made out to her for fifty grand.

"Oh my God! What is this for?"

"That is for you to get out of my grandson's life. It's yours clear and free."

Jemma's eyebrows shot up in surprise at the gesture. "You are joking, right?"

"No. You and Will don't belong with each other, and that check will make sure you stay away from him."

Jemma let out a deep breath, wondering why Mona kept harping on this. What business of it was hers that she had to keep sticking her nose into their lives? Jemma tore up the check and placed the paper on the coffee table in front of her.

"You've wasted your time bringing me this check. You're obviously super rich, but no amount of money will make me leave him."

Mona sighed as she shook her head. A small part of her glad that she'd have to use her visual evidence.

"If the money didn't sway you, this might. It was taken at the fundraiser last night." Jemma took the manila envelope, rolling her eyes, tired of Mona's antics.

She pulled the picture out, and her eyes got wide at what she saw. It was a damning sight, and her heartbeat increased at what she was looking at. It was a glossy eight by ten color picture of Will and Felicia kissing with his hands on her behind.

"This can't be true," she whispered as tears fell down her cheeks and Mona decided to twist the knife in further.

"From that passionate embrace, Will and Felicia are clearly an item. Just think, if my grandson was so in love with you, why is he kissing Felicia? You have to admit they do look good together," she finished with a malicious smirk, and Sonya had had enough. She stomped over to Jemma, snatched the picture, and shoved it at Mona.

"Get out of here!" Sonya demanded as she opened the door and

Mona left without saying a word, knowing she had accomplished her task.

"What an asshole," Sonya mumbled, walking back to her roomie. Jemma wiped her tears away as fresh ones fell from her eyes.

"Jemma, don't believe anything that old hag says. Will loves you; call him and find out exactly what happened last night," Sonya suggested softly, and she nodded. Jemma went to the bathroom to splash some cold water on her face after taking a few trembling breaths.

This was not the way she expected to start her day and hoped it didn't go downhill from here. She kept telling herself that it wasn't true, and Mona was lying because she had nothing else better to do. Jemma went to call Will; the knot in her stomach getting bigger when the phone wasn't answered.

"No one picked up," Jemma told Sonya faintly who was sitting beside her on the couch. "Do you want to go over there?" She nodded, and the two of them got dressed and walked over to the apartment. No one answered the doorbell and Jemma sighed deeply.

"He probably went out to breakfast with his brother or something," Sonya mentioned as they walked back home at a slow pace, trying to keep her friend's spirits up.

Jemma nodded; deep in thought. The weather was nice outside, and it promised to be a good day regarding the climate. Jemma couldn't even enjoy the niceness because she was thinking about other things. There could be a number of reasons why Will wasn't at home this early... He could've been out to breakfast. He might've gone for a run and went to go get his oil changed... Jemma knew she would keep trying to contact him and find out exactly what happened at the fundraiser. She knew Will would never cheat on her, so the sooner she talked to him, the better.

∽

THE MOMENT WILL WAS RELEASED from the hospital, he and Robert were on a task to find Felicia and wring her damn neck after getting answers from her. Will still couldn't believe that she had drugged him, and he wanted to know why. He'd never met a person like that before; to just do that out of the blue... He concluded that something was seriously wrong with Felicia and glad he never associated himself with her. Will and Robert had scouted all the usual student hang out spots and had even gone to her apartment, but she didn't show up in the few hours they had staked the place out. A few days later, Will was walking through the quad when Jemma ran up to him.

"Will! I've been looking for you!"

"Oh hey, babe." He looked tired, and he had bags under his eyes. Jemma knew she looked just as bad since she hadn't had a good night's sleep since Mona's visit.

"Why haven't you returned my calls?"

"I'm sorry. I've been trying to take care—" He stopped talking when Robert ran up to him with his book bag dangling from his fingers.

"I just saw Felicia walking into the drama building. Let's go!" They started to leave, but Jemma grabbed his arm.

"Will, stop! I—"

"Sorry, this can't wait!" he hissed, brushing her fingers away. She saw them run off; stunned about what had just transpired. Why did he run to go see Felicia? What was so important? Those questions were bouncing around her head as she headed back home with tears blurring her vision.

～

"He said that?" Sonya asked, sitting on the bed next to Jemma. They were in the latter's bedroom, and she nodded, using some tissue to wipe her nose.

"Yes. If nothing happened between them, then why did he run off to go find her?"

"This doesn't make any sense. Will is crazy about you."

Jemma shook her head as she let out a shaky breath. Her heart felt like it was in pieces. She'd trusted and loved Will and look what happened. She knew she didn't have all the facts, but the way he and Robert both took off let her know something had happened... something bad. Four days had passed since that ill-fated visit from his grandmother, and Will made no attempt to get in contact with her in any way. One would think that the first thing he'd do would be to talk to his girlfriend and explain the situation to her. She stood up and walked to her closet and pulled out her suitcase.

"What are you doing?" Sonya asked, standing up with wide, concerned eyes.

"I have to get out of here," Jemma replied as she pulled some clothes out her closet.

∼

A WEEK later after all the nonsense that happened with Felicia had ended, Will felt like he could breathe again. After confronting her, the brothers told Felicia they had a witness who saw her slip something into his drink and she had refused to talk after that. They had taken her to the police station and had told a detective of the events that happened. Robert had given Detective Andrews the name of the waiter who had seen what she had done, and he had followed up to get a written statement. Felicia was booked on charges of drug possession, and three days later, her pricy bond had been paid, but they didn't know by whom. He just wanted to get this over with and knew he'd have to testify if they ended up in court. Will knocked on Jemma's apartment door and Sonya appeared, scowling.

"What do you want?" she asked, crossing her arms over her chest and he looked at her with confusion.

"Um... hey, Sonya. I'm here to see Jemma."

"She's not here."

"OK, I'll wait for her."

"No, you don't understand. She left. Her aunt and Stan came and packed up her stuff."

"What the hell are you talking about?"

He pushed past her and stared in astonishment at Jemma's empty room; the only thing left behind was the bed and the dresser.

"Where is she, Sonya?" She was sitting on the arm of the couch, still glaring at him.

"I don't know."

"What's going on? Why did she leave?"

She shrugged, and he let out a low growl before walking out the apartment. He headed to his car, wondering what was going on. It wasn't like Sonya to have an attitude with him nor was it like Jemma to do something like this. He needed to find and talk to her right now.

～

"I'm sorry, Will. I promised I wouldn't tell you her whereabouts," Paris said, standing at the door, talking through the screen.

"Please tell me if she's here. I need to talk to her; it's important."

"She's not here. All I know is she called me crying last week about something and said she had to get away."

"But what if she's hurt or something?"

"I talked to her earlier; she's OK."

Paris felt bad for Will. She knew the two youngsters had to talk it out and fix whatever problems they had, but she promised Jemma she wouldn't interfere. Will let out a deep breath and placed his hands in his jacket pockets. He felt like punching a wall since he didn't know why Jemma had disappeared on him and felt frustrated because he couldn't talk to her.

"I'm not going anywhere, Miss Paris, not until I talk to Jemma."

For the next three months, Will kept his word, and when he wasn't in class. He was parked in front of Paris' house. Day after day, he waited, hoping she was lying, and Jemma would enter or leave the residence. On some days of his surveillance, Paris or Stan would take him food and beverages. At the end of the third month, after another day of no action, Will went home feeling dejected and empty. His usual feelings of exasperation were upon him again because things were left unsettled and unanswered between him and Jemma. He'd done a few pop-up visits at the apartment and knew her move out was real when Sonya had a new roommate weeks later. Glad his apartment was empty, he sat on the couch and tossed his head back. With his eyes closed, Will let out a deep breath as a single tear ran down the side of his face.

Check out Part 2 of Rutherford's Woman to see how Jemma's and Will's story ends

LIKE OUR PAGE

Be sure to LIKE our Major Key Publishing page on Facebook!

Made in the USA
Middletown, DE
03 May 2019